# The Cabin

# in the

# Deep Dark

# Woods 2

# The Cabin in the Deep Dark Woods 2

*The Spirit and the Bride*

**Tim Barker**

The Cabin in the Deep Dark Woods 2
Published by Tim Barker
Published in New Port Richey, FL 34654, U.S.A.
**All scripture is taken from the New King James Version®
unless otherwise noted.** Copyright © 1982 by Thomas Nelson.
Used by permission. All rights reserved.

Scripture quotations marked [NLT] are taken from the Holy
Bible, New Living Translation, copyright © 1996, 2004, 2007,
2013. Used by permission of Tyndale House Publishers, Inc.,
Carol Stream, Illinois 60188. All rights reserved.

Scripture quotations marked [KJV] are from the King James
Version of the Bible.
ISBN 978-1-951615-02-4
Library of Congress Control Number: 2021905574
Copyright © 2021 By Timothy L. Barker
Cover Design: Tim Barker
Original cover photo: Jon Sailer
Editor: Bonnie Olsen

# Dedication

This book is first and foremost dedicated to the Holy Spirit. Then secondly, it is dedicated to my wife Jilean, our four grown children and their spouses, and our grandchildren.

# Abstract of Principles

Repentance is an evangelical grace, wherein a person being, by the Holy Spirit, made sensible of the manifold evil of his sin, humbleth himself for it, with godly sorrow, detestation of it, and self-abhorrence, with a purpose and endeavor to walk before God so as to please Him in all things.

~ This quote is taken from The Southern Baptist Theological Seminary ~ 1858 ~ Number IX. Repentance

# Table of Contents

# Preface

I was inspired to write this series while listening to Jonathan Edwards's 1741 sermon *Sinners in the Hands of an Angry God.* Afterward, I thought, "Someone needs to write a story where God shows people who they really are from His perspective." That thought inspired me to write The Cabin in the Deep Dark Woods and then turn it into a series. In 1741 both Jonathan Edwards and George Whitfield preached that people must be born again. Whether or not you have been born again, this book will challenge your theology by opening the Bible, presenting God's truth to your heart.

In this book, I will take you on a journey through the Book of Romans. There are nineteen sections from Romans that became a part of this story and are listed below in the following format:

([1] Romans 1:16-17)       **Chapter 10**
([2] Romans 2:1-4)        **Chapter 10**
([3] Romans 3:23)         **Chapter 10**
([4] Romans 3:28)         **Chapter 11**
([5] Romans 4:23-25)      **Chapter 12**
([6] Romans 5:1-5)        **Chapter 12**
([7] Romans 5:6-11)       **Chapter 13**
([8] Romans 5:12-21)      **Chapter 14**
([9] Romans 6:1-10)       **Chapter 15**
([10] Romans 6:15-23      **Chapter 16**
([11] Romans 7:4-6)       **Chapter 17**
([12] Romans 7:7-12)      **Chapter 18**
([13] Romans 7:21-25)     **Chapter 19**
([14] Romans 8:1-11)      **Chapter 20**
([15] Romans 8:12-17)     **Chapter 21**
([16] Romans 8:37)        **Chapter 22**
([17] Romans 10:1-13)     **Chapter 22**
([18] Romans 12:1-2)      **Chapter 22**
([19] Romans 13:11-14)    **Chapter 22**

Saul's conversion in the book of Acts is just one example of an individual being converted from a life of sin to a life of grace in

Jesus Christ. Jesus questioned him while on the road to Damascus, asking, "Saul, Saul, why are you persecuting Me?" Then the Lord said, "I am Jesus, whom you are persecuting." It was clear from the passage that when someone persecutes Christians, they are actually persecuting the Lord Himself. Having lost his sight from the bright light, Saul was instructed to go into the city and wait. Three days later, a man named Ananias prayed for Saul, and he received his sight and was filled with the Holy Spirit, and after that, he was baptized. Immediately he began a life of preaching that Christ was the Son of God.

Thus the conversion of Saul was the beginning of the ministry of the Apostle Paul [Saul aka the Apostle Paul]. Today, many people are in the same situation as Saul from the book of Acts; they are going through life not being sure of their calling. However, most people have not encountered Jesus on a lonely road. This book is the story of a man who has refused forgiveness for a sin from his past. Grab your walking stick and come along on this journey where truth is the key to redemption. The road to redemption has many names: for Saul, it was Damascus. Have you found your road to redemption yet?

Acts 9:1-22

Thank you

Tim Barker

September 2021

# Acknowledgments

First of all, I want to thank my wife, Jilean Barker, for always being my greatest supporter. I also want to thank my mother and father for acknowledging the call of God in their lives, establishing a home with a foundation based upon Jesus Christ. I want to thank John and Annette Murray, who helped with the editing process. And finally, Bonnie Olsen, for her patience during her review.

Thank you all.

# About this Book

*The Cabin in the Deep Dark Woods 2* may be read several ways. First, like any book, front to back. Secondly, read each chapter and answer the discussion questions. Thirdly, read each chapter, answer the discussion questions, and review all scriptures listed at the end of the chapter or any way that you choose. Some of the Discussion Questions have answers provided and are denoted with the word (Answer).

You will want to pay particular attention to the following: *Without spoiling the story, italics are used to indicate a transition is occurring during the story that the character or characters are aware of. Italics are also utilized in the front matter and* **chapter 22 to indicate scripture.** **Bold type is utilized when something important is said or happens. It is used in some chapters as a subject header or a time transition header. You will also see bold type in the front matter to highlight a point.**

>Some chapters use offset indentation to tell a story or
>bring out a thought.

Next to most chapter headings, there is a day of the week, e.g. (Chapter 1 ~ Saturday). That chapter occurred on that day of the week. Whenever a day of the week is not shown in the chapter heading, that chapter occurred at another time. There are scripture references in parentheses at the end of some sentences and paragraphs, e.g. (John 3:16). This will allow you to verify the content of that sentence or paragraph. Some places have multiple references as the sentence or paragraph was detailed. When looking up these scripture references, check to ensure you are reading the correct passage if a connection CANNOT be made. **In this book, I will take you on a journey through the Book of Romans. There are nineteen sections from Romans that became a part of this story, listed in the Preface. They begin in chapter 10, end in chapter 22, and are in the following format: ([1] Romans 1:16-17).**

Throughout this book, quotations indicate that a character is speaking—colons (:) are utilized to indicate a long character quotation. Finally, all names used in this book are fictitious and are in no way implied to represent a real person.

This is a fictitious work, and in no way is it intended to override anything contained in scripture. All things contained in this book are superseded by the Bible. After you finish this book, I strongly encourage you to read your Bible, beginning in the book of John. And please don't forget to use this book as a study guide. It may also be used as a family devotional or a group study. I hope you enjoy your stay at the Cabin in the Deep Dark Woods. Please be sure to visit again by reading the other books in the series. These stories revolve around the same places in Edwardsville: the cabin, the mine, and the ranger station.

*The Cabin in the Deep Dark Woods—A Discerner of the Heart.*
*The Cabin in the Deep Dark Woods 3—Lost in the Way.* Release date late 2022.

**Other books by the author:**
*Ye Three Men—You are an Epistle of Christ.*
*Ye Three Men Devotional Edition: Devotional with Scripture.*

Thank you for purchasing *The Cabin in the Deep Dark Woods 2.* As a special gift, I would like to send you a free PDF of the *Non-Believer's Challenge*—a sixty-day study. To receive your free copy, send an email to:

**TheCabin@turnifyouwill.org**
**TheCabinInTheDeepDarkWoods.com**
Thank you
Tim Barker

# Chapter 1 ~ Saturday

# On a Hill Far Away

*M*arcus *looked into the man's eyes and said to him, "You have to get up now; it's just a little further." The man continued to struggle with the weight of his burden. At that moment, Marcus realized the prisoner wasn't going to make it up the hill on his own. He was resting on one knee and trembling while the sweat dripped from his brow. Then the prisoner looked Marcus in the eyes, piercing his soul. "Who are you?" Marcus asked him in a whisper.*

*Frozen in thought for a moment, Marcus felt the sweat fall from his own brow. Knowing he wasn't going to receive an answer, Marcus looked deep into the eyes of the man he was about to execute and asked him, "What have you done to deserve this fate?" He was beginning to sense that this may be an innocent man. Unable to help him, Marcus winced in pain as this man's cross slid ever so slightly, pressing the crown of thorns further into His scalp. The prisoner struggled with His balance, trying hard to keep His cross from falling to the ground while still resting on one knee.*

*As the moments passed in silence, another soldier riding a horse yelled, "MARCUS! KEEP HIM MOVING!" Marcus dug deep into his soul, gaining the necessary strength to carry on.*

*Soon, Marcus found someone to carry the cross for Him. This man also struggled while the two men stood and lifted the cross, resting it on their shoulders. It was heavy and awkward to move, dragging behind them, digging into the sand and gravel. While they pressed on, a cloud of dust trailed behind them. Some ridiculed the prisoner, and others struck Him. Some offered Him wine, which He refused. Yet, even others worshiped Him in a mockery; all the while, He pressed on. Then the prisoner spoke to the women who were mourning and lamenting Him, saying, "Daughters do not weep for Me" (Luke 23:28).*

*The two men collapsed in exhaustion when they finally reached their destination. As they lay on the ground, the cross rested on them. The other soldiers pulled the two men from underneath it, helping them to their feet. Then standing on His own, the prisoner willingly laid Himself on the cross.*

*Marcus once again found himself looking into the eyes of this Man. However, this time, he had a nail and a mallet in his hands. Then pressing the nail firmly against the condemned Man's flesh, Marcus raised the mallet and with a series of swift blows...* BANG—BANG—BANG! "Andrea! Andrea, are you in there?" yelled Janet MacArthur, Andrea's mother, while she pounded on her daughter's bedroom door. Then Janet shouted, "The service should have already started!" Andrea was confident that she had set her alarm clock the night before. Janet banged on her daughter's bedroom door once again. BANG—BANG—BANG! "Andrea! Andrea, do you hear me! Wake up! Wake up, girl! We need to get to the church. Everyone is there waiting for you." As Andrea woke from her dream, she looked at her clock, realizing that she should be standing at the altar looking into the eyes of her groom. Panic set in as she again heard her mother yelling from outside her door, "Andrea, where's your dress? We need your dress! Do you hear me? We need to leave now!"

Wearing only one flip-flop and carrying her wedding dress on one arm with her high heel shoes and make-up bag on the other. Andrea ran to the car where her mother was waiting with her foot on the break. Janet sped off before Andrea could even shut the car door. Andrea said, "Mom, you need to—Ugh—oh, Mom, that was a big pothole—slow down!" "Slow down! You are late for your own wedding and you want me to slow down!" Janet said. "Mom... "Don't mom me! There are over a hundred people at the church waiting for us!" Then Janet looked at her daughter, while taking her eyes off the road, and said, "You have less than five minutes to get your wedding dress on." Then as she turned onto the main highway, she hit a curb, losing a hub cap while blowing through a four-way stop sign.

After Andrea put her wedding dress on, Janet turned the car sharply into the church parking lot. Andrea held on for dear life as she put on her high-heeled shoes. At the same time, the tires slid across the pavement, sending out a screech, announcing to the guests in the sanctuary that the two women had just arrived. Janet put the car in park, and Andrea grabbed the rearview mirror to check her make-up one last time. Holding her wedding dress off the pavement, the two women ran to the church. Racing through the covered walkway, Andrea said, "Mom, I need to talk to you about a dream I had this morning." Almost sprinting, they approached the foyer door, where a man held it open for them. Inside, Andrea saw her father, Kenny Michaels; just then, the pipe organ began to play. Andrea's father asked, "Are you ready, Dear?" Extending his arm and locking arms with her, he escorted her to the altar. Then partway down the aisle, while looking back at her mother, Andrea said with her eyes, "I need to talk to you."

A few minutes later, Andrea said, "I do." "Well, son, you may finally kiss your bride," the minister said. Andrea's husband leaned in and kissed his beautiful wife.

Later the two women finally got a quiet moment to talk at the reception. Janet said, "Andrea, we may have gotten off to a late start, but that sure was a beautiful wedding." Then she asked her daughter, "So, Mrs. Peterson, what is it that you so desperately wanted to talk to me about?" Once again, the two women were interrupted, but this time by the tapping of the crystal glassware, so the bride and groom kissed one more time.

**Discussion Questions:**
1) Where in the Bible do you find passages that discuss marriage?

Answer: Genesis 2:18-24, I Corinthians 7:1-16, Hebrews 13:4, Ephesians 5:22-33, Colossians 3:18-19, Mark 10:6-9, Ecclesiastes 4:9-12, Song of Solomon 6:3.
2) Can you locate a few passages in the Bible where the crucifixion of Jesus is described? Hint: Look in the Old Testament as well as the New.
Answer: John 19:17-37, Psalm 22:1-21, Isaiah 52:13-53:12. There are others if you care to dig deeper.
Scriptures: Luke 23:28.
Discussion Question Scriptures: Genesis 2:18-24, I Corinthians 7:1-5, Hebrews 13:4, Ephesians 5:22-33, Colossians 3:18-19, Mark 10:6-9, Ecclesiastes 4:9-12, Song of Solomon 6:3, John 19:17-37, Psalm 22:1-21, Isaiah 52:13-53:12.

# Chapter 2 ~ Sunday

# Mr. and Mrs. Peterson

Mr. Peterson asked, "Mrs. Peterson, are you about ready?" "Almost Mr. Peterson," replied Andrea. The newlyweds were both giggling at calling themselves Mr. and Mrs. Peterson that morning following their wedding. They were getting ready to head out to the Cabin in the Deep Dark Woods for their honeymoon.

The company that Mr. Peterson worked for, Wesley Brothers Construction, had a contract with the state parks department to work on the abandoned mine and the surrounding area. They had been working on this project for the last several months and were almost finished. With the deadline fast approaching and Mr. Peterson being the superintendent, the President of the company, Jack Bradford, had decided to put the couple up in the Cabin for two weeks. It's known as the Cabin in the Deep Dark Woods. That's what they call it at the construction company. It's actually called the Cabin in the Way, part of a larger piece of property that belongs to the state parks department. Mr. Peterson would lead the construction crew during the first week, and the second was reserved for the newlyweds' honeymoon. Andrea was not okay with this arrangement until Mr. Bradford decided to pay for their stay at the Cabin. When she didn't smile right away at the meeting, he quickly added, "And I'll provide all the food as well." Mr. Bradford knew how valuable Mr. Peterson was to that project, so he was determined to keep Andrea happy. Andrea was looking forward to doing some reading and hiking in the woods, a week by herself, some alone time, as she called it. Knowing after almost a year of wedding planning, she could use it.

"The truck is packed. Are you ready, Honey?" Andrea heard the question, but her mind was drifting back to her dream of the man who nailed the hands of Jesus to the cross. "Where would this dream have gone if Mom wouldn't have interrupted?" Then she thought of the mallet hitting the head of the nail and whispered, "His eyes, it wasn't only Marcus' eyes that Jesus pierced; it was mine as well." Thinking more about the dream, she realized when Marcus looked into the eyes of Jesus, he saw the essence of holiness and the purity in His Spirit. "What I saw was hope, faith, and love," she thought.

BANG-BANG-BANG sounded a knock on her door. "Andrea, can you hear me? We need to go," Mr. Peterson said. Realizing she was once again back in that dream, she said, "I'll be ready in just a minute." Rushing over to the mirror, she put a beautiful white bow in her hair. Coming out of the bedroom, her husband looked at her and said, "You look lovely; now we need to go." He picked her up, putting her over his shoulder, and carried her to the truck. She giggled all the way, kicking her feet like she was really trying to escape.

As they pulled out of the driveway with a trailer in tow, Andrea took a good look at her beautiful new home with the white picket fence outlining the front yard. She began to daydream about the children they would one day have and maybe a dog and a cat too. She was confident that a great life lay ahead for them, but another thought raced through her mind. Looking back at a time in her life when she was devastated by her parents' divorce, she thought, "How will I ever break that chain?" Then, returning to reality, she pressed the thought of her parents' divorce out of her head. Looking over at her husband, she said, "There's nothing a girl likes better than taking the company pick-up truck on her honeymoon." "Your right," he said, adding, "but you have to admit, not every girl gets to use the company credit card to buy all the gas." Andrea smiled, thinking how lucky she was to have married such a good man.

Several hours later, the Petersons arrived at the Edwardsville Ranger Station. Mr. Peterson had to check in with the staff to complete the reservation paperwork. "Honey, isn't it beautiful out here?" Mr. Peterson asked. Andrea began to take in the beauty of her surroundings, seeing the mountain tops that seemed to go on forever. "Andrea, I'll be a little while checking in if you want to go for a walk," he said. Just then, her phone rang. "Not much chance of cell service up hear Ma'am," one of the park rangers said, adding, "you might want to take that call."

Saying, "Hello," as she answered her phone, noticing it was her mother who was calling. After a few moments of small talk, Janet asked, "What was it you so desperately wanted to talk to me about at your wedding?" Andrea went into detail, telling her mother everything that happened in her dream. Then she said, "Mom, the man who nailed Jesus to the cross in my dream was Marcus." Janet interrupted her daughter sharply, saying, "Let me be clear with you, young lady, I know a good man when I see one, and Marcus is a good man. Don't begin to doubt your husband, especially on your honeymoon." Then Janet began to describe her first meeting with Marcus at the restaurant that day by saying: "Remember he was the last one to the table because he helped that elderly woman up after she fell in the parking lot, tripping over a parking curb. Her family had to cancel their dinner reservation with her because of a family emergency. It was Marcus who brought her to our table to have dinner with us. Andrea, do you remember what day that was?" "Yes, Mother, I remember; it was Mother's Day." "That's right, Dear, it was. I remember crying on my menu and thinking that Marcus is a very good man. And don't you forget that this week!" There was a long pause, and Andrea said, "Hello—hello—Mom, are you there?" The same park ranger walked by and said, "I've never seen anyone get cell service up here before."

Just then, Marcus Peterson walked out of the ranger station. Looking at his wife, he said, "Andrea, are you ready to head to the cabin now?" Looking up from her cell phone, she noticed that the ranger had loaded all the luggage and equipment onto the John Deere and hooked the trailer up to it while she was talking on the phone.

## Discussion Questions:

1) If you were to look into the eyes of Jesus, what would be the outcome of that encounter?

   Answer: Isaiah 6:1-7, Daniel 10:1-9, Revelation 1:9-17.

2) Are you aware that Jesus died on the cross for your sins? Try explaining your eternal status with the risen Savior if you reject being born again.

   Answer: Romans 8:1-11, John 3:17-21, Psalm 50:16-23.

Discussion Question Scriptures: Isaiah 6:1-7, Daniel 10:1-9, Revelation 1:9-17, Romans 8:1-11, John 3:17-21, Psalm 50:16-23.

Scriptures: none.

# Chapter 3 ~ Sunday

# The John Deere

Wearing his sunglasses, Marcus was standing in front of an old hardwood bench on the ranger station's wrap-around front porch. Andrea took one look at her new husband and thought, "Wow, Mom's right as rain; that sure is a good man." "Honey," Marcus said, as he walked her way, "are you ready? Our ride is about to leave." "Hop on up here, Ma'am, Ranger Lucas Ward at your service. Welcome to Edwardsville. I'll have you two love birds to the cabin in less than five minutes; it's about a twenty-minute hike if you choose to walk." Marcus helped Andrea into the back seat.

"HOLD ON TIGHT," Lucas said. He pushed the gas pedal all the way to the floor, saying, "I hope you don't mind going fast!" Then he hit a pothole while leaving the ranger station parking area. Andrea had a flashback of her mom driving her to the wedding yesterday morning. Holding on for dear life, she remembered her mom hitting that pothole. Andrea thought, "My mother must have taught this man how to drive!" Over the noise of the motor, Lucas yelled, "I know this place like the back of my hand." Referring to the fact that he had been a ranger for the state parks department for many years and knew every trail backward and forward. Then he said, "You can always count on me." And turning around while driving, he began talking to Andrea, saying, "Ma'am, we're taking the second marked trail to the cabin. If you look over there, you can see one of the adits." Then he negotiated a sharp curve, hardly slowing down. Then he explained, "An adit is an entrance to the mine. Over there is one of the discarded rock piles from years gone by."

Continuing with his tour, Lucas said, "Up ahead is the red covered bridge. The creek sure is getting high this spring; it should crest sometime tomorrow. We gotta be careful around the creek," Lucas warned. Continuing his speech all the way to the cabin, explaining in detail the third marked trail that led to the abandoned miners' village. It ran along the creek bank, where some people had found ancient Indian relics, where the rocks were, while on their way to the miners' village. "We are on the straightaway now and will be at the cabin soon," Lucas yelled as he was driving through an open field at top speed. Lucas said, "Yes sir, I'm a praying man; I gotta be the way I drive around these trails. The Lord has kept His hand on me over the years." A few minutes later, Lucas said, "Well, it looks like we are here." He parked the John Deere by the stone wall attached to the front of the Cabin. "Over there is the first marked trail. It leads to the cabin parking area on Sandrock Creek Boulevard," At that, Lucas completed his self-imposed tour guide session of Edwardsville.

Andrea walked into the cabin and noticed how plain it was, all open except the bathroom. Lucas entered the cabin with her luggage and noticed how disappointed she looked. He told her that the cabin had been built as a church many years ago. He said, "It was not finished until the town of Edwardsville decided to make it into a one-room schoolhouse years later. Now it's this quaint little cabin out here in the middle of nowhere." Lucas realized that he hadn't made the idea of staying there any better for her, so he headed back outside to help Marcus.

"Let me help you," Lucas said while Marcus unhooked the trailer from the John Deere. "Boss, I'll be back here bright and early tomorrow morning to pick you up," The two men said goodbye and shook hands. Then he got back in the "Deere," at least that's what Lucas called it, and sped off.

Andrea walked out of the cabin to where Marcus was securing the trailer and said, "Honey, does anyone else know that man drives like a maniac. It's a wonder he didn't kill us." Looking at her watch, she said, "And we've only been married for twenty-one hours." Marcus responded, "I know, but he's my right-hand man on this project. If it wasn't for his knowledge of the property, we would have had to postpone the wedding. He is worth his weight in gold to me." "Well, then it's a good thing he's a little man because we couldn't afford him if he were any bigger," Andrea said while turning around to go back into the Cabin. Marcus asked, "What are your plans for tomorrow while I'm working with the crew?" "I think I'll go for a walk and see what kind of trouble I can get myself into." Then she asked, "Why don't you spend the day with me?" tempting her new husband to call in sick. Marcus said, "You know I can't do that, but it's really tempting as he chased her to the front door of the cabin, where she stopped. Marcus instinctively picked up his beautiful new wife and carried her across the threshold. Placing her back on her feet, he kissed her and confessed his love to her.

Later that evening, Andrea was unpacking her bags, and she took out her yellow hiking hat and hung it on a hook. Marcus said, "Honey, are you really going to wear that silly yellow hat around here? "Why yes I am; this is my favorite hiking hat. I'm sure you will come to love it just as I do," Andrea said. Then she thought, "Marcus, do you believe in God?"

All was quiet at the Cabin in the Deep Dark Woods. However, a couple of men wearing hooded cloaks with their faces concealed, having glowing eyes, kept a watch over things outside.

**Discussion Questions:**

1) "Yes, sir, I'm a praying man," Lucas said. How is your prayer life? When was the last time you prayed to Jesus? Have you set a standard in your life to get alone with God at a place and time where there are no distractions or interruptions? Have you kept to a standard praying daily, seeking the guidance of the Holy Spirit according to II Corinthians 3:3? ...written not with ink but by the Spirit of the living God.

2) Can you locate any scriptures in the Bible on prayer?

Answer: Psalm 102:17, Romans 12:12, Acts 2:1-4.

Note: there are many more scriptures on prayer if you care to seek them out.

3) Lucas pointed out some signs that said, "marked trail." A marker gives an indication of where someone will end up. What are some of the markers in your life? Do any of them provide you with peace and joy in the Holy Spirit? See Romans 14:17.

Scriptures: none.

Discussion Question Scriptures: II Corinthians 3:3, Psalm 102:17, Romans 12:12, Acts 2:1-4, Romans 14:17.

# Chapter 4 ~ Monday

# The Rocks Cry Out

While Andrea slept, she was awakened by the sound of the speeding John Deere zooming by the front of the cabin. Andrea said, "Marcus, you need to do something about that man and his driving; it's not even 6:30 yet!" "Honey, I gotta go. I'll see you tonight," Marcus said as he kissed her goodbye. "Hey! You didn't tell me where you're working today," Andrea said. She sat up in bed, anticipating an answer. "We are going to be working on one of the rock piles on the other side of the ranger station," Marcus said as he gave her another kiss before he walked out the door.

"Good morning, Boss. Is that little lady still sleeping?" Lucas asked. From inside the cabin, Andrea yelled, "Not anymore, thank you very much!" However, neither of the two men heard her. Marcus and Lucas walked to the John Deere, and Andrea overheard Lucas ask, "Boss, where do you want to go first?" After the two men drove off, Andrea could not get back to sleep. She rose to the aroma of freshly made coffee that blended perfectly with the fresh mountain air. Andrea thought, "How nice of Marcus to make me coffee this morning."

After two cups of coffee and a filling breakfast, Andrea laced up her hiking boots. She had decided that it was the perfect day to hike down to the abandoned miners' village. "I sure hope I can find some kind of ancient artifact to remember this trip by," she thought. Before long, she had crossed the red covered bridge making her way down the third marked trail. Soon, she saw what she thought was an ancient Indian arrowhead close to the creek bank between some rocks. Then carefully making her way to the water's edge walking on the rocks, she reached down to pick it up. Disregarding Lucas's warning the day before about the dangers of the rising creek with its fast-moving water, she slipped on a wet rock falling into the creek.

Over at the construction site, Marcus oversaw his crew of seven personnel while clearing out an abandoned rock pile. Suddenly, a man wearing a hooded cloak walked up behind him and said with the voice of holiness, "Behold, the rocks cry out." Looking behind himself and seeing no one, Marcus yelled, "ANDREA!" Hearing the desperation in his voice, Lucas ran over to the John Deere. Looking at Marcus, he exclaimed, "THE CREEK! WE NEED TO GET DOWN TO THE CREEK!"

"HOLD ON TIGHT," Lucas yelled as he raced the John Deere past the ranger station toward the red covered bridge. Then he turned onto the third marked trail toward the abandoned miners' village. Parking the John Deer, the two men dismounted and ran down to the creek where the water was raging. Marcus yelled, "That's Andrea's yellow hat, oh my God, she's in the water!" Lucas shouted, "Get back in the Deere; I know where she's going to land!" The two men sped off in the direction of the main highway. Lucas grabbed his radio and said, "Ranger Lucas Ward to base." Base replied, "Base here, Ranger Ward proceed with your message." Lucas said, "Base, we have a possible Signal 7 in the creek. Send all available personnel to intercept at the Sandrock Creek Boulevard Bridge." Base replied, "Base to all personnel, proceed to assist Ranger Ward at the Sandrock Creek Boulevard Bridge. This is an all-hands incident!" As Lucas hurried to the intercept point, Marcus asked him, "Lucas, what's a signal 7?" Lucas responded to his question by saying, "I know a shortcut down an unmarked trail. Hold on tight; it's going to get really bumpy!" The two men raced down a steep rocky embankment.

Afterward, Lucas turned the John Deere onto the main highway and said, "Up ahead is the bridge; that's where we're headed."

*While she floated down the creek, Andrea suddenly realized her feet were firmly planted on the ground. She was wearing a shiny white gown and was completely dry. She found herself standing in a beautiful warm garden and began to walk. She noticed various types of trees that she had never seen before. Soon, she heard a voice from behind her, saying, "Andrea, I am always with you and your children." Andrea turned around and saw a man walking toward her having a light emanating from his center like the glory of God. The man extended his hand toward her and said, "Andrea, come, take my hand and walk with me."*

*The man and Andrea walked through the garden for some time. Then He began to speak to her again, saying, "There are many trees in my garden that are pleasant to the sight and good for food. I want to inform you about those two trees that you see in the center" (Genesis 2:9). The man showed Andrea two trees that were straight ahead. Then he pointed to the beautiful one and said, "That tree is the tree of life, and all who eat of it will live forever" (Genesis 3:22). "I will be giving you instruction on the tree of life soon," the man said. "I have brought you here to talk to you about the tree that is next to it. It's called the tree of the knowledge of good and evil." While he was talking to Andrea, she was looking at the tree next to the beautiful one. She was puzzled and asked the man, "Why would anyone eat the fruit of that tree?" The man began to explain to her why she had been brought there, saying, "You see Andrea, your husband is eating daily from that tree. As the name implies, it is the tree of the knowledge of good and evil. Your husband is feeding on the good side of that tree. I will shortly give you insight about your children and how their lives will turn out while your husband, Marcus, continues to eat from the good side of that tree." Andrea asked, "But when will I receive this insight? The man said, "It will begin tomorrow morning, very early."*

*After they had walked in the garden for a fair amount of time, the man said, "Andrea, it is time for you to go back now." As Andrea looked down, she noticed that she was again wearing her*

15

*hiking outfit and soaking wet. When the man let go of her hand, she saw the nail print in His hand. Looking directly into His eyes, Andrea said, to Him, "You're the One that Marcus nailed to the cross in my dream, aren't you?" "No, Andrea, it was you. You were the one who nailed Me to the cross," the Man said while looking deep into her eyes. She felt more love emanating from this Man than she had ever felt before.*

*Suddenly, Andrea had this deep awareness that she could no longer breathe. Then the Man said, "Andrea, I have one more word for you regarding the tree of the knowledge of good and evil..." Andrea thought, "I really hope You hurry up because I am soaking wet, I am chilled to the bone, I can no longer breathe, and I feel as if I'm fading fast." Then the Man continued, "Don't look at the fruit of that tree, don't touch it, and don't eat it (Genesis 3:2-6). Andrea, do you understand what I have told you?" As He finished asking her that question, He moved ever closer to her until He finally placed His mouth on hers. Now holding her up with His arms because she had become entirely limp, the Man breathed the breath of life back into her lungs.*

Less than a minute after turning onto Sandrock Creek Boulevard, Lucas and Marcus arrived at the intercept point. Making their way down the embankment, they were the first ones to reach Andrea. She was lying face down on the sandy beach exactly where Lucas had predicted she would land. Marcus knelt down and embraced his wife, and then she opened her eyes and began to breathe again. Lucas caught a glimpse of the Man with the hooded cloak as He made his way back into the deep dark woods. Then, the Edwardsville Volunteer Fire Company number One arrived on the scene with the rangers and the construction workers.

**Discussion Questions:**
1) Can you think of something that irritates you but is not a sin, like how Lucas drives the John Deere?
2) Have you ever considered that Jesus knows all things? He even knows your future children, even before they are born? Although some people don't have children, most do. Can you

find in the Bible where it says God knows these children, even before they are born?

Answer: Luke 1:11-17, Jeremiah 1:1-5, Luke 1:26-33, Psalm 139.

Scriptures: Genesis 2:9, Genesis 3:22, Genesis 3:2-6.

Discussion Question Scriptures: see Discussion Question 2 above.

# Chapter 5 ~ Tuesday

# No Surprises

After the incident at the creek, Marcus brought Andrea back to the cabin, where she soon fell into a deep sleep. In the early morning, Andrea began to dream, and this is the dream she had:

*As he closed his eyes, Jason fired off all the rounds in his 9 mm handgun, and in a panic, he dropped it as he ran to the door, not even looking back.*

## The Night Before

*"Jason, are you sure you're ready to go through with this?" his best friend, Antwon Campbell, asked. "I'm cool; I got your back, man. You've got nothing to worry about with me," Jason said. Then he said to Craig Steel, "If you want to back out, now is the time. Tomorrow there is no turning back. Are you still in?" The three men looked at each other and said all together with a cheer, "I'm in!" Looking at the rough diagram of the Four Rivers Bank, they began to scheme a plan that would yield them enough money that they would never have to work again. Antwon, being the self-appointed ringleader, began to go over his notes of the bank, giving the details of each step that was needed to pull off that heist. Antwon said, "Craig, you bring the car—the one Jason picked up last week, Jason, you bring the ammo, and I've got the*

*firearms already here. I'll see you two back here in the morning at 7 o'clock sharp; oh, and no surprises."*

*As Jason Peterson was walking home that night, he thought about how he met Antwon and Craig. They met each other on the high school wrestling team, Craig was a heavyweight, but Antwon was the same weight class as Jason. The two had to compete for a starting position on the varsity team. By their senior year, the three boys were the team captains and formed a bond that is still strong.*

*As Jason entered his apartment, he hung up his key in the kitchen and walked over to his girlfriend, Debbie Johnson, who was sleeping on the couch, waiting for him to come home. They had planned to get married, but something prevented that from happening every week. Last week, they both lost their jobs. Jason knew they were both out of work, but he decided not to tell Debbie he lost his on the same day that she lost hers. "Hey, where have you been? I was beginning to worry," Debbie said after he kissed her on the cheek, waking her up. "I was out with Antwon and Craig; we are planning on going to Four Rivers tomorrow morning bright and early to do some bluegill fishing," Jason answered. Completely awake, Debbie said, "Okay, I'll go with you guys." Debbie went to the same high school as the three boys, and they all got pretty close during their senior year. The boys were expecting wrestling scholarships, but a series of unfortunate events and late-season injuries put a damper on those plans. Several years after high school, they still struggle to make a living in this one-stoplight town. "Jason, you look like a ghost. Did I say something wrong?" Debbie asked. In a moment of sheer panic, Jason said, "Sure, you can go fishing with us." Avoiding, for the time, the true nature of the event that was planned for the morning.*

*The next morning came faster than he had expected. He hadn't thought his way out of this predicament with Debbie thinking she was going fishing with them. He even put his fishing pole by the front door. Debbie was still sleeping when it was time to leave, so Jason tried to head out quietly only to knock over the pots stacked by his key in the kitchen. "Jason, are you trying to leave without me?" Debbie asked from the bedroom. "No, I was just putting* away the dishes," Jason said with a wince of pain in his voice that Debbie didn't catch. Soon, the two of them were walking to Antwon's apartment. Debbie said, "It's okay; we're going to be just a few minutes late—they won't shoot us, you know. Just relax and quit acting so nervous." Jason knew that Debbie would flip out when she discovered the truth. "Not only Debbie but Antwon and Craig," Jason thought.

While walking up the stairs, he felt as if gravity had increased four-fold, and his legs began to feel like they were filled with lead. He saw that Antwon's apartment door was open, awaiting his grand entrance. Jason knew those last few steps were the proverbial point of no return. With each step, Jason asked himself, "Am I courageous, or am I a coward?" He could not distinguish between the two. Nevertheless, he had crossed the threshold—his life would never be the same.

That next moment, when all eyes met, the tension was so thick, it was felt like a chill in everyone's bones. Gesturing to Jason's fishing pole, Antwon said, "This is sure a SURPRISE, isn't it, Craig!" Craig's silent stare into Jason's eyes sent an even deeper chill down Debbie's spine, warning her that something was wrong. "Jason, what's going on here?" Debbie asked while looking at both Antwon and Craig with a deep questioning stare. After a long pause, Antwon said, "Jason, that's YOUR question; we're already behind schedule." Jason finally admitted to Debbie precisely what the plan was. If Jason was ever right in his life, this was the day. Everyone was freaking out, and he was feeling the brunt of it. "This is no way to start a bank robbery," Jason thought. All the while, he wished his life would have sent him in a different direction.

After a few minutes of tense arguing and shouting, Debbie noticed three 9 mm handguns lying on the coffee table. She said, "Jason, what the frick are those doing there?" Without hesitating, Antwon reached over and grabbed one of the handguns from the coffee table. He pulled the magazine out and cleared the chamber. He said, "See, Debbie, there's no ammo. We aren't going to go into the bank with a loaded handgun; that would be stupid. Every detail of this job has been thought out—none of us will ever have *to work again." Then Antwon said to Jason and Debbie, "You two go home or get ready to go to the bank!"*

*Antwon said to Craig, "Big boy, I said Debbie is driving! We have five minutes until we will be at the bank—from here on out, everyone gets along!" As Debbie was driving them to their new favorite fishing hole—the Four Rivers Bank, Antwon said to Debbie, with a tone of authority, "Park over there, behind that bus." The three men got out of the car, each grabbing a backpack, and headed to the bank. "Dude, why did you want to park so far away from the bank?" Craig demanded. Looking at his watch, Antwon said, "Forty-two minutes behind schedule, and all you care about is where we parked the car!" Jason interrupted, saying, "Let's pull together and think positive—what could possibly go wrong?"*

*Emma Jackson gave Nolan Roberts a greeting just like she had done every weekday morning for the past four years. Emma said. "Good morning, Sir; every girl loves a man in uniform." Being many years older than Emma, Nolan was a father figure to the young bank teller. He always responded to her greeting by asking her, "Ma'am, are you the bank president yet?" Emma loved her job at the Four Rivers Bank, and she had a lot of confidence that Nolan was there every day as an armed security guard. Nolan was a retired law enforcement officer. He took his job very seriously and was never late—today, however, he was a little early.*

*The three men ducked into a small alley and behind a dumpster, loaded their handguns just as planned, now forty-five minutes behind schedule. Then entering the bank, Jason yelled, "STICK EM UP!" Antwon thought, "I can't believe he just said that!" Antwon belts out an order to his comrades, saying, "SPREAD OUT! Emma dropped her coffee as her world turned to slow motion. She began to raise her hands, hearing the sound of steel moving against leather as Officer Roberts drew his Glock from his holster and said, "DROP YOUR WEAPONS!" Craig instinctively looked at the man giving the order moving his firearm in the same direction as his eyes. POP—POP. Craig dropped to the ground. POP—POP. Antwon was hit in the abdomen and hand, dropping his weapon. As he closed his eyes, Jason fired off all the rounds in his 9 mm handgun, and in a panic, he dropped it as he ran to the door, not even looking back. Then Jason and Anton made their way back to the car.*

*Debbie, who was driving to nowhere, screamed, "WHAT HAPPENED? WHERE IS CRAIG?" Jason yelled, "SLOW DOWN! They don't know what we're driving—just be calm." "BE CALM! YOU WANT ME TO JUST BE CALM!" Debbie yelled as she hit a curb, losing a hub cap while turning onto the main street of town. "How's he doing?" Debbie asked. "His hands really bad, and he's lost a lot of blood," Jason said. Thinking how wonderful it would be to be sitting on the river bank with a bluegill on his fishing line. However, Jason's thought was interrupted by the siren of a police car responding to the bank. Debbie asked once again, "Where's Craig?" "He's dead," Jason said, not realizing what he actually told her until Debbie responded by saying, "OH GOD, OH GOD, YOU CAN'T BE SERIOUS!" "Get off the main road; they'll catch us for sure!" Jason said. Then he added, "We need to turn around and go to the hospital, or else Antwon's going to die too."*

*Shortly after, Debbie and Jason were in front of the hospital, soon realizing a high police presence surrounded the facility. Jason said, "I didn't think there were that many police cars in this town." "That's right—you didn't think, and that's the problem!" Debbie said, who was more disgusted than ever. "He's dead," Jason said. "I know, you said that already," Debbie said. Jason countered, "No, I mean Antwon is dead too." "Jason, you really know how to give a girl a great life, you piece of..." Interrupting her, Jason said, "Turn the radio on." Then the radio blared: "Breaking News Report: This is an update on the attempted robbery at the Four Rivers Bank this morning. There are reports that three men..." Debbie turned off the radio and said, "We just need to turn ourselves in!"*

*Then the phone rang in Andrea's dream, she answered it, and said, "Hello." A woman on the other end said, "Andrea, my name is...*

**Discussion Questions:**
1) Have you ever had plans, but they never seemed to work out like Jason and Debbie trying to get married?
2) Have you ever been in a situation like Jason where you were about to do something, knowing that the ones you love would be disappointed? Like with Jason and Debbie, where the actual event was a bank robbery rather than a fishing trip?
3) At any moment, a bad decision can change your life. One day you may need to press deep down in your heart of hearts and take a stand. Can you think of a time when you had to take a stand on an issue? What was the outcome? Did you make the right choice? Would you like to expand?

Scriptures: none.

# Chapter 6 ~ Tuesday

# The News Journal

Marcus said, "Andrea! Honey, you were dreaming. You need to wake up." Andrea said, "Our son, Marcus, where is our son?! He's in trouble! Our son is in trouble!" Marcus said, "Andrea, what are you talking about? You have been in bed since 3:30 yesterday afternoon. You haven't been up since I brought you back from the creek. It's now Tuesday morning at 2 o'clock. You were dreaming. Andrea, you need to get some rest; go back to sleep, Honey."

Andrea was puzzled. Remembering her encounter with the Man in the garden, she thought, "Now this dream about a son named Jason who robbed a bank with his friends." Laying back down in bed, she began to wonder, "What in the world is happening?"

BEEP—BEEP—BEEP. "Six o'clock sure came fast," Marcus thought as he shut off his alarm and dragged himself out of bed. Looking at his beautiful new wife, he looked to heaven, and with a tear rolling down his face, he said, "Thank you, Lord." Seeing headlights coming towards the cabin, Marcus thought, "I sure hope Lucas doesn't wake Andrea up this morning." Then Lucas turned the John Deere just before he got to the cabin and parked it. Marcus went outside to meet him. "Boss, I have to insist that you stay here at the cabin and take care of Andrea this morning. I'll be back later to pick you up. We really don't need you; we just make you think we do," Lucas said as he walked over to the John Deere and sped off.

It was mid-morning when Andrea finally woke up. What a surprise, she thought, finding her husband sitting by her bedside. The events of the previous day began to surface in her mind. Andrea sat up in bed and said, "Marcus, where did you find my yellow hat?" Marcus handed her the hat with an attached note. It said, "Ranger Lucas ward at your service, you can always count on me." She noticed some other writing at the bottom that she couldn't make out. Handing Marcus the note, she said, "It looks like he writes like he drives. Can you read the bottom?" Marcus took it, and looking closely, said slowly as he struggled to read Lucas' handwriting, "Yes—Ma'am—I'm—a—praying—man." Marcus explained all the events that transpired the previous day and how Lucas knew that she would end up on the sandy beach by the bridge. Amazed and overwhelmed, Andrea held her yellow hiking hat close to her heart and said, "You know, he's worth his weight in gold to me." Then Marcus took her yellow hat and said, "My dear, I have come to love your yellow hiking hat." "Marcus, I need to talk to you about a dream that I had the morning of our wedding," Andrea said as she sat up in bed. Just then, the sound of Lucas driving the John Deere filled the cabin. For the first time, it was a comforting melody to Andrea's ears. Marcus and Andrea greeted Lucas, and the three talked, enjoying a cup of coffee. Andrea thought how blessed she was that her husband was influenced by this humble man of prayer.

Later that day, while Marcus and Lucas were working on the same rock pile past the ranger station, another man wearing a hooded cloak walked up behind Marcus, whispering in his ear, "Where is Katie?" Spinning around, Marcus saw no one. He yelled to Lucas, "Where is Katie? Sensing Marcus was still shaken from the incident at the creek yesterday said, "Katie-Bird is in the valley setting posts for the new pavilion. She is helping Jim and Steve." Katie-Bird Lewis was Jim and Steve's sister, and she had joined them on this trip to get away from the city for a week.

Putting his arm around Marcus, Lucas said, "Boss, everything is okay here." The man wearing the hooded cloak disappeared into the deep dark woods only to reemerge on the cabin's front porch while Andrea was still inside.

Later, when Andrea walked out on the front porch with her freshly poured coffee, she saw a newsletter lying on the table in between the rocking chairs. Picking it up, she read the title, *The Way News Journal*. "Interesting," she thought and sat down to read.

**Discussion Questions:**

1)  Have you ever had a situation in your life where you didn't like something or someone? Then an event took place, and you had a change of heart. Like the relationship between Andrea and Lucas?

2)  Lucas left Andrea a note that said, "I'm a praying man." Do you have a prayer life? If not, today is the perfect day to start. Just set a few minutes aside daily and talk to God. Oh, and if you don't have anything to say to Him, that's okay. Just wait, and God will begin to speak to you.

Scriptures: none.

# Chapter 7 ~ Tuesday

# Don't Talk to Strangers

As Andrea was sitting in the rocking chair on the front porch of the cabin, she began reading from *The Way News Journal*, and this is the story she read:

*Katie realized that she had never seen any part of that town in the daytime. She wasn't sure if he was actually going in the right direction.*

## The Night Before

*It was a cold and rainy night. The tires on the bus were humming out a song in perfect harmony with the melody of the highway. Before long, the bus driver pulled into the last scheduled stop, a little diner in the middle of nowhere. He had driven that same route for many years and had it down to an exact science. He said in a monotone voice at the same moment he set the parking brake, "Twenty-five minutes—if you're not back in your seat, I'll see you back here this same time next week." He was trying to sound stern, but he's never left anyone behind yet.*

*"That will be $9.37," the cashier said. Katie replied, "Okay, just take off the iced tea. What will that be?" "Miss, that will be more; you ordered from the value menu," the cashier said. Katie said, "I only have..." Just then, an elderly woman from the bus placed a ten-dollar bill on the counter. "Ma'am, You don't have*

to do that," Katie said. The elderly woman said, "And you don't have to eat. If you were my daughter…" (Katie's mind drifted, for a moment, to her upbringing or the lack thereof.) "…I would insist that I buy your lunch." The elderly woman handed the money to the cashier.

Yielding to her kindness and taking her tray, Katie sat down at a table by herself. Soon after, the same elderly woman who bought Katie's lunch asked, "May I join you, Dear?" Having practically raised herself, even Katie knew that it would be rude to refuse someone a seat after they had extended an act of kindness. Katie said to her, "Of course, and thank you for buying my lunch." After setting down, the woman said, "My name is Marie." "Katie," she said while taking a bite of her cheeseburger with its stale bun. "Katie Peterson, my name is Katie Peterson." The two of them talked while they ate their lunch, and Marie began to get the feeling that Katie was running away from something, or someone, or maybe even both.

Twenty-one minutes after parking the bus, the driver put his dirty dishes in the dish rack and headed back to the bus. "We'd better go," Marie said. While picking up her tray, she said to Katie, "Save me a seat if you can."

Katie was one of the first ones back on the bus. Having her pick of seats, she took one close to the back by a window. Katie was hoping she could sleep for the next several hours. She was traveling light, having only these items in her pockets; a little cash, a comb, and her driver's license. Twenty-four minutes after setting the parking brake, the bus driver started the diesel engine as black smoke billowed from the back of the bus. Soon, the driver shut the door. As the bus slowly rolled out of the dirt parking lot, splashing through the mud, he turned on the windshield wipers. "A seat all to myself," Katie thought. After a few moments, Marie sat down next to her and said, "Thank you, Dear, for saving me a seat."

An hour later, Katie thought she knew everything about Marie there was to know. Realizing she wasn't going to get any sleep, Katie decided to join the conversation by answering Marie's questions. Katie said, "I'm heading to the city to get a fresh start *in life. Things at home were never the same after the divorce. I haven't seen my dad for the last six or seven years, and my mom hasn't been happy for about as long." The bus driver slowed as he maneuvered the bus into a tight turn. Marie said, "Well, it looks like we're already at the downtown station. After the bus stopped, Marie stood up and said, "Katie, I'll let you out." Marie took an envelope out of her purse, concealing it from Katie for the moment. "I thought you were getting off here?" Katie asked. "No, dear, there's nothing left for me to do in this town." Katie slid out past Marie, and then Marie handed the envelope to Katie. She said, "This is for you. I think you will need it more than I." Katie was beginning to realize how desperate her situation was. She took the envelope and turned toward the front of the bus. While walking away and looking down at the floor with a slight of shame in her voice, she said, "Thank you." Then Marie said, "Dear, I have one more thing to say to you." Katie spun around to listen, and Marie said, "Don't talk to strangers, don't get into a car with someone you don't know, and above all else, always let your parents know where you are." Katie paused for a moment acknowledging Marie's words, then turned and walked away.*

*As Katie stepped off the bus, she noticed right away how dark and cold it was. The rain was falling in a steady downpour, hitting her in the face. She began walking as the wind and rain persisted in letting her know that she was still miserable, and before long, she was drenched. About half an hour or an hour later, she could not tell how much time had passed since her shivering body and wet clothes consumed most of her thoughts, she arrived at a fleabag motel called The Grand Tranquil. She walked inside the office, asking the man behind the glass partition, "How much for a room tonight?" "Sixty-five," the man said without looking up at her. Shivering, Katie reached into her pocket, hoping the envelope Marie had given her contained enough money to get her through that night. Counting out the bills, she handed the man 70 dollars. Looking at her this time, he said, "That's 65 before the resort and sales tax." Reluctantly Katie paid the additional amount. Then with her room key in hand, she began looking for room 104 while the rain continued to fall. "It can't get any worse than this," Katie thought, all the while; she wished her life would have sent her in a different direction.*

*"Number 102, 103, oh, finally, room 104," Katie thought. As she put the key in the door, she said, "Yea, your right! 'You may have to jiggle the key a bit to open the door.' And I'm sure they are gonna fix it tomorrow." All she could think about was a hot shower, some heat, and a cozy warm bed. Inside the hotel room, it looked like it hadn't been cleaned in a while. The heater was broken as well. "That doesn't feel like it is blowing much heat to me," Katie said out loud. "I'll warm up in the shower," she thought. However, when she turned the hot water on, only nasty black and orange rusty colored water came out of the showerhead and at a fast-paced dribble at best. She debated if it would do her any good to go to the office and complain. Then she realized that all she had to claim that hotel room with was only a key since she wasn't given a receipt. She had handed over $73.45 in cash. "Besides, I'll just eat breakfast in the morning," she remembered the man saying that they would be serving a continental breakfast at 7 o'clock.*

*After laying her wet clothes out to dry, Katie got in bed and somehow managed to fall asleep. She couldn't decide which was worse: the shivering, having been wet and tired, or being away from home with only $23.55 in her pocket. She drifted in and out of sleep throughout the night. She even got up once and gathered all the towels and spread them out on the bed as additional blankets.*

*Around 7:30 the next morning, Katie was awakened by a man and a woman arguing outside her door. She thought she might as well get up and head to the lobby for some breakfast. Katie put her clothes back on, realizing they hadn't dried as much as she had hoped. "A free breakfast that will get me going," she said. Walking outside, she noticed it was colder than she had expected. Still, looking on the bright side, she said, "At least it's not raining anymore."*

*"Hot coffee, things are beginning to turn around," Katie thought as she tore into her stale blueberry muffin. While having her second cup of coffee, a middle-aged, overweight man walked*

*into the hotel lobby, where Katie was sitting at a table by herself. He poured himself a cup of coffee, then joined her by sitting down at her table. By then, Katie fit the profile, looking like a runaway. She was only 17, and she was a very attractive young lady. "The name's Joey. Are you going into town sometime today? I can give you a ride; my car is right outside," the middle-aged man said, who called himself Joey Something. Once again, Katie realized how dire her situation was. She looked at Joey and said, "I don't think that would be a good idea." All the while, she couldn't shake the advice that Marie gave her the previous night. "Don't talk to strangers,"*

*Katie thought, "What could it hurt to talk to him for just a few minutes?" "You sure are pretty; it wouldn't be any trouble to give you a ride. I'll even get you some real food at this nice little diner I know of," he said as he tried to convince her to go into town with him. "Okay," Katie said, reluctantly giving in to her hunger. Then Joey headed to his car with Katie following. Getting in, Katie once again played back those words that Marie said to her, "Don't get in a car with someone you don't know." Again, she pushed that advice to the back of her mind and put it with the first one.*

*Katie realized that she had never seen any part of that town in the daytime. She wasn't sure if Joey was actually going in the right direction. "How far to the diner?" Katie asked him as her hunger had been replaced with uncertainty. "Just around that bend," he said, not looking at her as he spoke. His demeanor had transitioned into a flat stare, looking straight out the windshield displaying no emotions. Then, that overweight middle-aged man abruptly turned the car onto a dirt trail leading to who knows where. "Why did you turn off the road? Where are you taking me?" Katie asked as Marie's last warning flashed in her mind: "Above all else, always let your parents know where you are."*

*Then, while a cloud of dust trailed behind the car, an angel stood before Katie's Heavenly Father... "Take heed that you do not despise one of these little ones, for I say to you that in heaven their angels always see the face of My Father who is in heaven—Matthew 18:10."*

**Discussion Questions:**

1) After reading Matthew 18:10, and this News Journal, what do you think about those people who have hurt, taken advantage of, or worse—murdered one of God's little ones? Whether they were a child or an adult.

2) "All the while, Katie couldn't shake the advice that Marie gave her the previous night." Thinking back on that advice, at what point did Katie make a bad decision?

3) When was the point of no return regarding Katie having no control over the situation?
Answer: the first mistake—talking to Joey at her table in the lobby. The point of no return—getting in the car with Joey. Once these first two mistakes were made, Marie's final piece of advice was no longer of any value.

4) When is the best time to (always let someone know where you are)? It would have been better if this piece of advice had taken place before the first two.

5) Uncertainty. This word was used after Joey had a change of demeanor. Uncertainty comes to our mind in degrees of measure. At first, it is light and just a warning, then more and more until it may be too late. Can you think of a time in your life when uncertainty was speaking to your heart or mind?

Scriptures: Matthew 18:10.

# Chapter 8 ~ Tuesday

# The Fruit of That Tree

S till sitting on the front porch of the cabin in her rocking chair, Andrea could hardly put down that first edition of *The Way News Journal.* Reaching over, she picked up her coffee, and finding it to be cold, she thought, "Wow! I didn't see that one coming." As she wiped the tears from her face, she remembered her dream of Jason and the encounter with Jesus in the garden. "Now," she thought, "this news journal article about a daughter named Katie. I think two children will be plenty." Just then, *The Way News Journal* vanished right before her eyes. Getting down on her knees, she began to pray. She remembered Marcus saying to her, "I can count on one hand the number of times that I have been to church, including our wedding." "Dear God, I ask you to guide me through this journey called marriage and family. Instill in me the knowledge and wisdom needed to guide my husband, enabling him to feed our family from the tree of life. I am ready and willing to listen to you, Lord God." Andrea began to contemplate how she would explain *The Way News Journal* to Marcus.

Shortly after Lucas assured Marcus that nothing was wrong at the job site, the crew broke for lunch. They headed down to the pavilion leaving the two men alone for the first time since the accident at the creek the previous day. As the last of the crew disappeared from sight, Marcus put his hand over his eyes and began to cry. The weight of what could have happened to Andrea fell on him like a tidal wave of bricks. Lucas instinctively placed his hand on Marcus' shoulder and said to him, "It was by the grace of God that Andrea's life was spared. If that were my wife, I would be getting alone with God in prayer and ask Him, why did this happen?" Then turning to face him, Lucas said, "One more thing, Boss, why did you want to know where Katie-Bird was?" Remembering the voice he heard, Marcus scratched his head, and while walking away, he said, "Never mind."

Still on her knees praying, Andrea began to weep in a manner unlike any she had ever experienced before. It was as if she were crying in her spirit and speaking directly to Jesus. She began to wonder if this was the godly sorrow she had heard about back in her church days (II Corinthians 7:10-11). It was a deep cry, seemingly coming from her center. And then, she remembered a discussion that she had with Jesus during her encounter in the Garden. "Why hadn't I remembered this before now?" Andrea thought as another part of that encounter came back to her memory:

> While Andrea was walking in the garden with Jesus, she asked Him, "Why would anyone eat the fruit of that tree?" Jesus said: "Andrea, there are many reasons why people eat the fruit of the tree of the knowledge of good and evil, but the main reason is they haven't been born again. Andrea, you were born again when you were a child. You read your Bible and even prayed more than most people. That all changed when your parents divorced. You drifted away from Me, and I allowed you to do that for a time, but I am a jealous God. Now I am drawing you back to Me. I have shown you what will happen to your children if Marcus is not born again. Jason can be a successful young man, and Katie, a talented young woman. If Marcus isn't born again, he will only be able to feed his family from the corrupt nature of the tree of the

knowledge of good and evil. And we both know how
that will turn out. Don't think your husband doesn't
love you; he loves you very much. Andrea, your
mother is right about him; he is a very good man. All
that needs to happen is…

Interrupting her prayer, Marcus asked, "Andrea, what's
wrong?" He had returned to the cabin and saw Andrea on her
knees, praying in godly sorrow. "What?! What needs to happen?!"
Andrea shouted, then she realized that Marcus heard the question
that she had intended for Jesus. "Marcus, I was just praying,"
Andrea said. "I've never seen anyone pray like that before,"
Marcus said. Andrea asked, "Marcus, I've been thinking, have
you ever been born again?" "Katie, don't be ridiculous! I came
back to the cabin to see if you were all right, and you ask me if
I've ever been saved?" Looking up at him, Andrea said, "Marcus,
you just called me Katie!" "No, I just called you Andrea. I'm
certain of it," Marcus said. Andrea asked him, "What does Katie
mean to you?" She noticed that question seemed to strike a chord
with her husband, and she did not want to make it snap. She
thought that moment was the right time to open up to him, and she
began telling him all that had happened since the morning of the
wedding. So, at that, they began to talk about the dream where
Marcus nailed Jesus to the cross. The encounter in the garden with
Jesus as a result of her falling into the creek. And her insight of
Jason and Katie from the dream and *The Way News Journal*.

As the newlyweds came to the end of their discussion, Andrea
began to question God, asking Him, "How am I going to lead my
husband to know God, all on my own?" Just then, the sound of
the John Deere approached the cabin as Lucas sped by the front.
Then Andrea heard those words play out in her head one more
time: "Ranger Lucas Ward at your service, Ma'am."

**Discussion Questions:**
1) Lucas said to Marcus while the two men were alone: "If that
   were my wife, I would be getting alone with God in prayer
   and ask Him, why did this happen?" Have you had a situation
   in life that warranted getting alone with God seeking an

answer on how to handle a problem? If so, what was the outcome?

2) Have you ever experienced godly sorrow in your life or witnessed a loved one being in godly sorrow?

3) Jesus said to Andrea, "There are many reasons why people eat the fruit of the tree of the knowledge of good and evil. But the main reason is that they haven't been born again." What are you feeding your life, spiritual or worldly food?

Scriptures: II Corinthians 7:10-11.

Discussion Question Scriptures: none

# Chapter 9 ~ Wednesday

# Faith

Andrea waved as Lucas and Marcus sped off in the John Deere that morning. They were about to begin this project's main objective: clearing out the mine from the collapse that occurred many years ago. Today the crew will start the task of re-establishing Edwardsville's very own mine railroad system. However, Andrea was deep in thought as she pondered how her husband would eventually come to know God. She walked out onto the front porch and noticed another edition of *The Way News Journal* sitting on the table, in-between the two rocking chairs. "Well, here goes," she thought. Andrea knew she had to read what was in this latest edition.

*My dearest Andrea, my name is Abraham. Early one morning, I heard from the Lord. He says to me, "Abraham, take your son Isaac and go and offer him as a burnt offering to Me." So, I took Isaac and two of my men. We split the wood for the burnt offering and loaded it onto a donkey. After that, we began our journey to the place that God had told me of. We traveled for three days, and then I saw the place up ahead and said to my men, "Stay here with the donkey. Isaac and I will go and worship, and we will come back to you." So, I took the wood for the burnt offering and had Isaac carry it. I took fire in one hand and a knife in the other, then the two of us went together.*

At that point, Andrea wiped the tears from her eyes, for she was familiar with this passage, she even knew how it ended, but that day was different. It was as if Abraham somehow told her how he felt about this act of faith.

*As my son and I walked, he asked me, "Father, here is the fire and the wood, but where is the lamb for a burnt offering?" I said to him, "Son, God will provide for Himself the lamb for a burnt offering." So, we walked on, soon, arriving at the place where God had told me to go. There I built an altar and placed the wood in order, and then I bound Isaac, my son, and I laid him on the altar, upon the wood.*

Andrea noticed that the news journal became tear-stained right before her eyes. She felt anguish and godly sorrow in her spirit like Abraham was feeling at this occurrence. This was no longer a story to her but more like a personal account from a close friend.

*Andrea, this next part that I tell you, I want you to understand where my heart was. It was secure in my faith in God that His word is true and sure. I had told the two men that Isaac and I would soon return. I believed this in faith as I recalled the words of my God repeatedly in my heart and mind:*

> *"Sarah, your wife, will bear you a son, and you will call his name Isaac. I will establish My covenant with him for an everlasting covenant, and with his descendants after him (Genesis 17:19).*

*Then I raised my hand with the knife to slay my son, knowing that the promises of God were sure. But the Angel of the LORD called to me from heaven and said, "Abraham, Abraham! Do not lay your hand on your son; for now, I know that you fear God since you have not withheld your son, your only son Isaac, from Me." Then I looked up and saw a ram caught in some brush by its horns. So, I went and took the ram and offered it up for a burnt offering instead of my son Isaac (Genesis 22:1-13).*

*Andrea, you must understand one thing, all that needs to happen is for you to have faith in God, and He will do the rest.*

*Just as I had faith in Him, you must also have faith that He will answer your prayer that Marcus will be saved. Can you imagine what was going through my mind as I walked for three days with my son? I was deep in prayer to God, never wavering from my faith. Once I even said to God, "Father, all that I have at this moment is my faith in You that I will return my son to his mother." Andrea, always pray for your husband in faith, believing that He who has begun a good work in your husband will complete it (Philippians 1:6).*

*Your friends in faith,*
*Abraham and Sara.*

Once again, the news journal disappeared right before Andrea's eyes. Then, she remembered her dream of Jason robbing the bank, specifically the end where she answered the phone call and had a conversation with Marcie Johnson. And this is what she remembered from her dream:

> "Andrea, you don't know me, but my name is Marcie, and my daughter's name is Debbie Johnson." Marcie went into great detail, explaining to Andrea all the events that transpired during the bank robbery and those that happened shortly after at the police station. The two women talked for a long time. By the end of the conversation, in her dream, Andrea had a great urgency welling up in her spirit that the root cause of the situation was a direct result of her failed marriage and the lack of her son having a Godly father figure in his life.

The words of *The Way News Journal* crashed back into her mind, *"Andrea, always pray for your husband in faith, believing that God will be able to perform it."* Andrea began to pray that God would make a way so that Marcus would become a man of faith and prayer.

At the ranger station, Marcus met with Lucas and the construction crew about the upcoming tasks that were to be completed in the mine. Marcus gave the following presentation to the construction crew members, saying:

"The mine had been used as storage by the townspeople of Edwardsville. Many years ago, there was a cave-in, which buried a time capsule stored in there. Inside the time capsule are three items; however, all records of those items were lost during the same cave-in.

The three mine technicians are Jim, Steve, and Katie-Bird Lewis. They are leading the shoring operation in the mine, giving us the needed protection all the way to the time capsule.

The steam engine and train repair technicians are headed by Keith Harmen and his two assistants, Jacob and Noah Foster.

The three train track technicians are Jeff Davis, Cliff Russel, and Jeff's wife, Clair. They are amateur train hobbyists specializing in laying miniature train tracks. They should be arriving soon, but Marcus noticed that they were late.

Our objectives are to get the mine railway system back up and running. We will remove the iron gate so we can begin to shore up the mine. Ultimately haul out the 100 feet of rocks and six boulders, freeing up the time capsule before the annual Edwardsville community dinner this Saturday night. There is a lot of work that needs to be done for us to reach our goal, but we can do it."

After the meeting, Marcus had Jim and Steve go to the cabin with the John Deere to pick up the trailer that had the workbench and tools needed for this phase of the project.

**Discussion Questions:**

1) The offering of Isaac in Genesis 22 is an extreme example of obeying the voice of God. Can you think of any other occurrence in scripture where someone else gave up their child?

   Answer: I Samuel 1:19-28, Exodus 2:1-10, John 3:16.

2) In Genesis 22:5, Abraham said to the men accompanying him, "Isaac and I will go and worship, and we will come back to

you." Where in the Bible is the measurement of Abraham's faith described?

Answer Hebrews 11:17-19.

3) Have you ever, out of necessity, had to give up something dear to you, such as a car, a house, or even a job that you loved?

Scriptures: Genesis 17:19, Genesis 22:1-13, Philippians 1:6.

Discussion Question Scriptures: Genesis 22:1-19, I Samuel 1:19-28, Exodus 2:1-10, John 3:16, Hebrews 11:17-19.

# Chapter 10 ~ Wednesday

# Make His Paths Straight

Andrea noticed the John Deere driving to the cabin—a lot slower than usual, "Hum," she thought, "what's up with Lucas driving so slow all of a sudden?" Then she noticed it was Jim and Steve. As Jim got out of the John Deere, he said to her, all the while looking at Steve, "Steve was driving," indicating why they were going so slow. "We're here to get the trailer," Steve said to Andrea, ignoring Jim's statement. "Well, you two boys go right ahead." Andrea was heading out to go on another hike. "Be sure to stay away from the creek," Jim said. Andrea turned around and gave him a wink. Then she adjusted her yellow hiking hat, indicating she wasn't going to do any more swimming.

Jim and Steve hooked the trailer up to the John Deere, then headed over to the adit—the entrance to the mine. In the trailer were all the necessary items to repair the locomotive and the train carts. The locomotive's steam engine had developed a steam leak in one of the cylinders that only worsened with time. The mining company was on the verge of bankruptcy when the cylinder finally gave out. Since there were no funds available to make the repair, the locomotive and train carts were just set aside. That was until Edwardsville obtained a grant, which funded that project. There was enough money to purchase specialty equipment and parts to make the repairs and the expert personnel to perform the needed work.

As the John Deere arrived at the adit with the trailer in tow, Marcus and Lucas were heavy into a discussion. "Are you certain that Keith can fix the locomotive? It's been sitting there for ages," Marcus said. He pointed to the small train sitting on the remains of the mine track in front of the mine's entrance in a sad state of disrepair. "He was highly recommended by the parks department, so we need to have faith that he can get this old train up and running," Lucas said. Then adding, "It reminds me of a passage from the book of Romans where the Apostle Paul said, 'The just shall live by faith.'" "Okay, but what does that have to do with getting an ancient train running by Friday?" Marcus asked. "The Bible says that the gospel of Christ is the power of God to salvation. So, as we have faith in Jesus Christ for salvation, we too must have faith that God will also meet our needs during this project," Lucas responded. Marcus listened to his words and placed them in the back of his mind where they wouldn't interfere with this construction job. ([1] Romans 1:16-17).

Andrea was hiking along the first marked trail when she started singing a song that came into her heart:

A little bit of worship
—a little bit of praise
Praise His holy name—I say
Praise His holy name
Jesus—Jesus
A little bit of worship
—a little bit of praise
Sing His holy name—I say
Sing His holy name
Savior—Savior
A little bit of worship
—a little bit of praise
I am calling You—I say
I am calling You
Jesus—Jesus
A little bit of worship

—a little bit of praise
I am praising You—I say
I am praising You
Jesus—Savior
Praise Your holy name—I say
Praise Your holy name

Andrea sang that song as she walked along the first marked trail. She was also praying for Marcus, speaking the name of Jesus over his need for salvation.

She hiked to the main parking lot out on Sandrock Creek Boulevard. Once there, she noticed the mailbox with the address 1224 Sandrock Creek Boulevard written on the side. She thought, "That sure is a sad-looking mailbox. I should check to see if there is any mail." She opened it, looked inside, and pulled out another edition of *The Way News Journal*. A few steps ahead of her, out of view, another one of those hooded men passed by. Before she opened the news journal, Andrea closed her eyes and said, "Please, please, please, Lord, no more children—those two are going to be enough for me." With the news journal in hand, she sat down on a parking curb and began to read.

*My dearest Andrea, I am a man sent from God. My name is John, John the Baptist. I am a witness to the Light of God so that all people may believe. I was not that Light but was sent as a witness. This Man was the true Light who gives inspiration to everyone that comes into the world. He was here on this earth, and the world was created by His mighty works. But the world did not know him. He came to His own people, who would not receive His word. But those who receive Him, those who believe in His name, He gives the right to become children of God. Those people are the ones who are born of the Spirit of God. Andrea, our heavenly Father, is drawing your husband to the Son of God. Be strong in your faith.*
*Yours truly, John.*
*"The voice of one crying in the wilderness:*
*'Prepare the way of the LORD;*
*Make His paths straight.'"*
*(John 1:6-13 & Matthew 3:1-3)*

Andrea was not shocked that she came across another one of those news journals. Still, she was puzzled why this one didn't disappear when she finished reading it like the others had. So, she just tucked it into her back pocket, forgetting about it for the time being.

When Jim and Steve arrived at the adit, Keith gruffly demanded, "It's about time you two got back with the trailer. Help us get the workbench and equipment un-loaded!" Keith was a world-renowned steam engine mechanic, and he was one of the most helpful guys you could ever meet. Though that day, Keith was under a lot of stress. He had been tasked with overhauling that locomotive in a shorter than usual amount of time. He quickly got to work on the old pup, as he called it. It was a lot smaller than the railway systems he was used to working on. He had also studied the train's logbook, isolating the problem down to one of the steam cylinders. He thought he could have it up and running fairly quickly.

"Hey, I'm sorry I yelled at you two guys," Keith said. Steve looked at him and said, "It's a good thing you toned it down a notch, buddy, or you would be unloading this trailer all by yourself." Jacob and Noah—Keith's two assistants, who had been working on the three train carts, began to assist with the trailer and help calm him down a bit. Marcus seeing the commotion, stepped in to help. Jacob and Noah were setting the tone for hustling. Jacob had been a preacher in a life gone by. Now he tinkers with old trains in his retirement, and his younger cousin Noah has been tagging along these past several years. Once Jacob set the pace for the younger crew members, he set his cruise control to steady as he made sure they kept chugging along. As the others began to tear into the cylinder, Jacob saw that as an opportunity to take a break.

"Hey Boss, this old train reminds me of a message that I preached once on repentance," Jacob said to Marcus. Andrea always said of Marcus, "He has the gift of listening." Jacob continued: "Keith was pretty hard on those two good old boys a few minutes ago. God's word teaches us that we are not to judge others on their actions because we bring the same condemnation on ourselves. I've seen it time and time again—one man throws a fit, and another man acts like he's never done anything wrong in his entire life. For example, take that incident back there; once Keith said he was sorry, Jim and Steve jumped right in and helped him unload that trailer. Now, look at them go; they're running on all cylinders. God's judgment is all about truth. What Keith did was a small example of repentance. I say small because it wasn't some big sin. He just threw a fit for a minute and then said he was sorry. Steve didn't hesitate to accept his apology, thus extending forgiveness to a typically humble man." ([2] Romans 2:1-4).

Tap—Tap—Tap. "I think that will do it," Keith said to everyone. Jacob may have been acting like he was on a break, but he and Marcus had gotten the scrap wood ready for the test run of the newly repaired locomotive steam cylinder while they talked. There was a lot of excitement in the air as the fire began to heat up the steam boiler. Soon the water was boiling, and Keith opened the main valve giving power to the drive wheels. "It's moving," yelled Noah as he had never seen a mine railway locomotive in action before. Lucas walked up and said to Marcus, "I think the crew is motivated to meet our goal. "Okay, that's good—shut her down," Keith said because there were only thirty feet of usable track in place that day.

Noah was a young man, and being the youngest of his family, he had lost his way about five years ago. That's when Jacob decided to get involved in his life. There was a great generational gap between the two men as Jacob was more of a grandfather to Noah than a cousin. Jacob didn't look at that situation like he had left a congregation of 400; instead, he looked at it like he had acquired a congregation of one. Lucas asked, "Noah, did I hear Jacob say that he was a preacher?" Noah had gotten used to telling the story about his troubled past, how Jacob gave everything up to mentor him. "Yes, he stepped down as the senior pastor of Cedarwood Congregational Church after 38 years," Noah said. Noah had lost his desire to be prideful after his troubled years, especially after his cousin Jacob jumped into his life, giving up everything for him. Noah continued by saying, "Jacob was a Holy Spirit-filled preacher always emphasizing the need for the baptism of repentance." Jacob could always sense when Noah was telling someone his story. The older gentleman always gave him leeway to share his testimony.

"Hand me that crowbar and sledgehammer," Noah said to Lucas. The two men were working on the work carts pulled by the mine locomotive. The wheels had rusted over time because the mine railroad system had been sitting neglected for years. "I'm not sure if we are going to be able to get all these wheels working," Noah said. Keith had assigned him to recondition the wheels, twelve in all. "Lucas, these wheels are ancient, and nobody makes them anymore. If we're going to use this mine train, we have to get them working again. We may even have to weld them back onto the work carts," Noah said. He had gotten good at working and talking after receiving the Holy Spirit—a gift from God, Jacob always said. Lucas and Marcus helped with the cart wheels while Noah told his story:

"Between the ages of 12 and 15, I lost my way in life, finally ending up at a juvenile detention center. I never shot or hurt anyone, but I had this desire to steal. I just needed stuff. It started out simple enough; I would steal snacks and drinks from the Quick Mart. Then I moved on to stealing alcohol and cigarettes. Finely, I moved on to stealing to pay for my drug habit. I thought I knew what I was doing. That is, I thought I was smarter than everybody else. Then I double-crossed these two guys one day, and they ratted me out and set me up good. I was supposed to steal a car for them. However, it was a setup, and I got caught. This got me sentenced to two years behind bars in the state penitentiary. My cousin Jacob visited me every week during those two years. At first, I cried in my self-pity, but later I cried over Jacob's sacrifice. I had my first Bible placed in my hands on his first visit. Jacob said to me, 'Son, I think it's time you look at what God has to say about your life before you throw it away.' I was still a little too hard-hearted to open that Bible. Then on his next visit, he asked me,

"What passage have you read?" It was the fire in his eyes that pierced something inside of me. I knew that when he came back to visit, I had better be able to quote at least one Bible verse. I opened the Bible in my cell late that night, after crying in self-pity, to Romans 3:23 and read, "For all have sinned and fall short of the glory of God." ([3] Romans 3:23)

Then for the first time in my life, I felt how far my life was from the glorious nature of God. As I thumbed through the Bible, reading other passages, I began to notice how much time Jacob had spent in his Bible. There wasn't hardly a page that he hadn't highlighted, underlined, or had written a note in the margin. All I knew about the Bible was that there was an Old and New Testament. Knowing that most people only read from the New Testament, I flipped Jacob's Bible to the Old Testament, which had also been studied over. Then checking the front presentation page, it had been given to Jacob by his father just before he died. I noticed it had a recent date where it was presented to me.

> *To: Noah Foster, my son in Christ Jesus.*
> *I John 1:9 If we confess our sins, He is*
> *faithful and just to forgive us our sins and*
> *to cleanse us from all unrighteousness.*

I don't know exactly when I gave my life over to Jesus. It was sometime before the third visit as Jacob pointed his finger at me and looked me in the eyes, and said with a grin, 'You've been reading from Romans, haven't you?' I never answered him, with words, that is. I just looked down, and the tears flowed from my eyes like a river. After that visit, I read Jacob's Bible every day for hours upon end. I even read all the way through Leviticus, falling asleep and having to re-find my place, but I read all of it. I made it through the whole Bible in less than six months."

Jacob and Keith walked over, seeing the three men working on the cart wheels. Jacob said to Noah, "It looks like you got one wheel working—only eleven more to go," Noah gave the older man a big smile, having received approval from him once more.

As he started working on the second cart wheel, Noah said, "It was my sins that nailed Jesus to the cross." Marcus dropped the crowbar and remembered the words he said to Andrea when they discussed her dream: "Well, it sure wasn't me who nailed Him to the cross." "Are you okay, Boss?" Lucas asked. Once again, Marcus looked a little shaken as he said, "Fine, I'm fine." But this time, that story hit him in a direction that he wasn't expecting. Somehow it left a mark, and it even stung, but Marcus wasn't sure where he felt it yet.

BANG—BANG—BANG! The second cart wheel fell off as Marcus, for the moment, felt himself in Andrea's dream, nailing Jesus to the cross. Focused once again, Marcus picked up that second cart wheel and set his mind to restore it. Then he said to Noah while he was walking over to the workbench, gesturing with the cart wheel by raising it over his head, "I've got this one, Noah!"

**Discussion Questions:**

1) *A Little Bit of Worship—a Little Bit of Praise*: That was the song Andrea sang while she walked along the first marked trail. Can you find any songs in the Bible?
   Answer: Psalm 96, Psalm 40, Psalm 48, Relation 5:8-14.

2) The Bible says that the gospel of Christ is the power of God to salvation. It takes faith to believe that statement. Have you put your faith in Jesus Christ, believing in the power of the gospel?
   Answer: Romans 1:16-17, Galatians 2:16, Galatians 3:11-12, Hebrews 10:38, I John 5:10-13.

3) Noah said in this chapter, "It was my sins that nailed Jesus to the cross." Where in the Bible can this be confirmed?
   Answer: Romans 3:23 For all have sinned and fall short of the glory of God.

4) What is the answer to sin? (found in this chapter).

Answer: I John 1:9 If we confess our sins, He is faithful and just to forgive us our sins and to cleanse us from all unrighteousness.

Scriptures: Romans 1:16-17, Romans 2:1-4, John 1:6-13, Matthew 3:1-3, Romans 3:23, I John 1:9.

Discussion Questions Scriptures: Psalm 96, Psalm 40, Psalm 48, Relation 5:8-14, Romans 1:16-17, Galatians 2:16, Galatians 3:11-12, Hebrews 10:38, 1 John5:10-13, Romans 3:23, I John 1:9.

# Chapter 11 ~ Wednesday

# I'll Take the Faith Route

A ndrea walked along the second marked trail, which led to the red covered bridge. While crossing the bridge, she found another edition of *The Way News Journal* nailed to a post. Taking it down, she began to read.

*But now the righteousness of God apart from the law is revealed, being witnessed by the Law and the Prophets, [22]even the righteousness of God, through faith in Jesus Christ, to all and on all who believe. For there is no difference; [23]for all have sinned and fall short of the glory of God, [24]being justified freely by His grace through the redemption that is in Christ Jesus, [25]whom God set forth as a propitiation by His blood, through faith, to demonstrate His righteousness, because in His forbearance God had passed over the sins that were previously committed, [26]to demonstrate at the present time His righteousness, that He might be just and the justifier of the one who has faith in Jesus (Romans 3:21-26).*

"That's great," Andrea thought, "but I have never used propitiation in a sentence in my entire life. What does that word even mean?" She looked at the bottom of the page, and it said: *"TURN OVER."* So there on the back of the news journal was this statement:

*Andrea, it is I who justifies the wicked through their faith in Me (Romans 3:26). I am the propitiation (Romans 3:25). I cover the sins of the sinner with My blood. It is the sacrifice that I made on the cross of Calvary in My death, the death of the last Adam, who became a life-giving spirit (I Corinthians 15:45). I am that second man, the Lord from heaven (I Corinthians 15:47). I am the propitiation for the sins of the whole world (I John 2:2). Have faith; My blood was shed as a propitiation for a covering of sin: yours, your children's, and that great sin of Marcus that he still carries in his heart.*
*Your Savior*
*Jesus*

Again, the news journal disappeared after she finished reading it like the others had. Then she checked her back pocket, finding the news journal from John the Baptist still there from earlier. Andrea said silently, "That's it; I'll just have to have faith that God will make a way for Marcus to come to know Jesus as his Savior." She asked herself, "What could be eating at my husband that would preclude him from accepting the saving grace of Jesus Christ?"

BeeP—BeeP—BeeP went the delivery truck as it backed up to the mine entrance. Noah yelled to Marcus, "Hey Boss, I think the delivery guy needs you to sign some paperwork for him." The truck driver said, "I just need you to sign my delivery sheet for the rail track." Marcus walked over and signed the paperwork laying aside his project, leaving the second cart wheel on the workbench, the one he was fixing for Noah. "Five-hundred feet of mine railway track should be enough to finish this project," Marcus thought while he walked to the ranger station to file the delivery sheet. All the while, he was thinking that amount of track may be cutting it short. Marcus remembered his boss, Mr. Bradford, saying to him, "Just don't make any mistakes with the track." He was making an emphasis on the fact that the rail track was a special order from overseas. It was a relatively large chunk of the cost of the entire project.

"That should do it," Jeff said as the last piece of track was unloaded from the delivery truck. Jeff, Cliff, and Jeff's wife Clair were amateur train hobbyists specializing in laying miniature train tracks. They had met Keith at a steam engine convention a few years ago and had worked on several other small projects since. Still, this one was by far more significant and involved.

Lucas saw the brand-new rail track and noticed it wasn't stacked appropriately. So, he said to Jeff and Cliff, "You two guys need to re-stack those rail-track pieces, so they don't fall over?" Then, Lucas noticed Jeff's T-shirt and said, "Jeff, I don't believe your shirt is appropriate. You will need to change it." So, at that, Jeff and Cliff began the process of re-stacking the rail track. This time to the standard that Lucas held them to.

While Lucas was heading to the pavilion for his morning prayer time, he passed Marcus on his way back from the ranger station. Lucas said to him, "I told Jeff to change his shirt. It's not appropriate to have that kind of sexually explicit and derogatory depiction of a woman displayed while working around the ranger station. It reflects poorly on this establishment and the other rangers." Marcus had noticed the T-shirt earlier, but it didn't bother him.

Afterward, Lucas was spending his morning break, looking over a devotional study from the book of Romans at the pavilion. Marcus walked over to the work station at the mine entrance, and he examined the rail track that had just been re-stacked. He said to Cliff and Jeff, "Great job, guys." He didn't know that Lucas had just made them re-stack it. Then as Marcus was walking away, he remembered what Lucas said to him moments ago. He turned around and said, "Hey, Jeff, I'm going to have to ask you to wear something more appropriate from now on." Jeff began to voice his disapproval of Lucas's opinion of his T-shirt. Knowing that Lucas had prayer time down at the pavilion every morning, Jeff fired back sharply, saying to Marcus, "Did that little Bible-thumping twerp complain about my shirt?" Marcus had seen worse clothing displayed on other job sites; however, Jeff struck a chord when he called Lucas a little twerp. Spinning around once more, Marcus, in a commanding tone, while pointing his finger in Jeff's face, said to him, "You have one minute to change!" Jeff hadn't made it known to anyone that he was hurting for money, not even Claire.

Jeff hadn't taken on this project as a hobby but somewhat out of necessity. Jeff quickly headed to the ranger station to change his shirt because he knew Marcus had the authority to fire him on the spot.

After reading the news journal, Andrea was still standing on the red covered bridge. Claire was also taking advantage of the nice weather and taking a little hike of her own. Claire saw Andrea on the bridge. She stopped and said, "Andrea, you're such a lucky woman to have a husband like Marcus." Both women were still on the red covered bridge when Claire asked, "So, Andrea, where are you headed?" Without receiving an answer yet, Claire said, "I'll just tag along." Andrea thought, "Okay, you'll just tag along then." Andrea was just beginning to be deep in thought about her most recent news journal article. She was about to question God concerning her dream of her future son Jason and the *Way News Journal* story of her future daughter Katie. "You know Andrea," Claire said, "my husband has been drinking a lot these past few months. That's why I say you're a lucky woman." Claire was a lot older than Andrea, being in her late 40s, and she looked like her marriage to Jeff had been a hard life. Andrea being a younger woman, was not expecting to be counseling anyone this early in her marriage, especially someone much older. As the two women walked along, Claire began to tell Andrea more about her life and marriage than she could possibly want to know.

Lucas was sitting alone at the pavilion, having his morning devotional time. He thanked God for the time he had with his wife before he lost her in an accident years ago. He was still reading from Romans. While he finished up his study, Andrea and Clair were heading to the miners' village. They happened to see him sitting at a picnic table and stopped to greet him. Andrea, being one of Lucas's biggest fans after her accident at the creek, asked him what he was studying. "I'm reading from Romans chapter three, where it says that man is justified by faith apart from the deeds of the law." ([4] Romans 3:28). "Well, what does that mean?" Claire asked. At the same time, she sat down across from him, joining herself in on his devotional study. Lucas said, "It means that it is our faith in Jesus Christ that saves us rather than trying to follow the law of Moses and the ten commandments." Claire said, "Yep, that would be pretty tough. I'll take the faith route." Then she asked Lucas, "So, what do I need to do?" Lucas and Andrea looked at each other at the same time. Lucas saw Claire yesterday when she, along with Jeff and Cliff, arrived at the ranger station and were late for Marcus' briefing. That was the first time he had actually met her. After the incident with Jeff earlier, Lucas had just assumed that Claire would be like her husband. Now, he thought otherwise. So, after praying with Lucas and Andrea, Claire kneeled down and began to pray this prayer to God as she had been ready to turn her heart and life over to Jesus Christ for a long time:

> "Lord, I lift up my soul, and I will trust in You. Please take my shame from me. Show me Your ways and direct my paths. Lead me in Your truth and teach me, for You are the God of my salvation. Do not remember the sins of my past. I come before You in my humility. I know your ways are mercy and truth. Forgive my sins, for they are numerous. I have come to feel a great fear of the Lord. I turn my eyes to you; show me your ways. Turn Yourself to me, and have mercy on me, for I am lonely and worried. The troubles of my heart have increased; bring me out of my despair! Look at my difficulties and my hurt, and forgive all my sins. Keep my soul, and deliver me; let shame pass from my life, for I put my trust in You. Let integrity and Your righteousness preserve me out of all my troubles! You are my Redeemer and Savior; in You and You alone, I put my trust." (Derived from Psalms 25).

Lucas handed Claire his handkerchief. Then she stood up, wiping the tears from her eyes and face as the words of her prayer were spoken through her sobbing. This was a prayer of the destitute, one that God will not despise (Psalms 102:17). Andrea thought, "Wow, I sure miss-judged her." All the while, Lucas was having the same thought flowing through his own mind. "I should let you get back to work," Claire said to Lucas. Then the two women turned and walked away, leaving Lucas somewhat speechless but grateful and joyful in his spirit.

"Andrea, I think we were heading to the miners' village," Claire said. "Yes, I think your right," replied Andrea as they continued on their hike by way of the creek. This time it was no longer a raging rapid. Soon they passed the small rock pile by the creek, where Andrea had her mishap the other day. They continued on to the miners' village for some needed exploring.

Back at the mine, Noah continued to work on the train's cart wheels. He was tackling wheel number six. Jacob said, "Looks like your almost halfway there, little cuz." Lucas was catching up on some duties at the ranger station seeing the crew was focused on meeting their goal for the time being. Keith continued his restoration of the miniature steam locomotive. Jacob had decided to take another one of his self-appointed breaks. He walked over by the pile of rail-track. "Let me give you a hand with that track Jeff," Jacob said. The three men: Jeff, Cliff, and Jacob, began to layout the track. Steve, Jim, and Katie-Bird started the task of cutting the lumber for the shoring operation. This was needed for the stabilization of the mine drift. This was to prevent any more cave-ins while the time capsule was removed. Most everyone worked in silence except for Jacob, who was singing praises to the Lord. This pace continued throughout the remainder of the day until quitting time. Marcus looked around the job site, thinking that nothing could stop his crew from reaching their goal on time. "That was a superb effort by everyone today," Marcus said as the workday had finally come to an end.

Soon after, Lucas arrived at the job site to take Marcus back to the cabin, where Andrea had prepared dinner for the two men. Later as the three of them ate their dinner, Lucas was unusually quiet and out of character. Marcus thought that he was quiet because of the confrontation with Jeff over his T-shirt that day. Andrea thought he was quiet because he was still thinking about Clair's prayer at the pavilion earlier. After dinner, the three of them were sitting on the front porch taking advantage of the cool mountain breeze. Andrea brought out some coffee and apple pie. She said to Lucas, "This ought to cheer you up." Lucas was fiddling nervously, stirring the cream around in his coffee. Looking up, he began to unfold one of his most endearing secrets. Lucas said: "It was ten years ago today that my wife Caroline drowned in a surfing accident. It wasn't like I could forget about her, but when you almost drowned in the creek, Andrea, all my memories and feelings came rushing back. I prayed for her in that hospital for countless hours, but in the end, God called her home. Marcus, I can tell you that I prayed hard for Andrea while driving you to the sandy beach down by the bridge. I loved my wife very much, and I miss her even more. You're a blessed man Marcus. You're such a blessed man."

That was a moment Marcus hadn't planned for. A man opening his heart about a tragedy from his past. Yet, he still professes the greatness of God's love upon his own life. "What was it about this man's faith that drove him deeper and deeper into the love of God?" Marcus thought. Then Marcus asked Lucas, "What got you through it?" Lucas answered: "It was my dad's perseverance in his faith that taught me to find strength in Jesus Christ. My dad was a preacher; his book of choice was Romans, and he preached a powerful message on faith every Sunday. My dad would consistently preach on faith throughout my growing-up years. Although my faith was shaken in Caroline's death, it remained firm in the end. My dad said to me one day, 'Lucas, it was your prayer life that got you through Caroline's death.' It wasn't until after my dad died that I began to realize how much faith I really had in Jesus through my prayer life. It was after Caroline's death that I felt the call to become a ranger. My father was called to the pulpit, but I was called to the great outdoors."

Later that night, just before Andrea drifted off to sleep, she began to question God. What could have prevented her son from wanting to rob that bank in her dream? She also asked, "What could have prevented my daughter from running away from home in the news journal article?" However, Marcus was more than a little shaken at realizing that Lucas had lost his wife to a drowning accident. Still, he was more shaken that his own wife was spared. "What could this possibly mean?" he asked himself, or so he thought, but he was really asking God.

**Discussion Questions:**
1) What does *propitiation* by His blood mean in the context of Romans 3:25?
   Answer: Propitiation is a covering of sin by the blood of Jesus. Further from Exodus 25:21, "You shall put the mercy seat on top of the ark, and in the ark you shall put the Testimony that I will give you.
2) Mercy is [an attribute of God] whereas mercy seat is [a covering], and the testimony is [a witness]. Thus, propitiation can be understood as: Jesus is your witness. He has offered a covering for all your sins by the word of His testimony. He confirmed this by the shedding of His blood on the cross at Calvary. By accepting Jesus as your savior, you agree to allow Him to instruct you daily through His Holy Spirit by having a personal relationship with Him in prayer. Has this happened in your life?
3) Read Psalms 25:10 & 18, Psalms 102:17, and II Corinthians 3:3. Consider saying your own prayer from these verses. Here is an example: All Your paths Lord, are mercy and truth to all those who keep Your covenant and Your testimonies. Now look on my affliction and my pain, and forgive my sins. I know You will regard my prayer and not despise me because I am destitute. I have placed all my faith in You, Jesus. Have Your way with me and cover me with Your righteousness. Cause me to keep Your ways Oh Lord by writing Your law on my heart, not with ink but by Your Spirit, not on tablets of stone but on tablets of flesh, that is, on my heart. I humbly plead with You, Oh God, as I have become broken and tender-hearted. Revive my spirit within me, and I will cling to You all the days of my life. Amen and Amen.

   Are you willing to be humble following after Jesus in faith?
Scriptures: Romans 3:21-26, I Corinthians 15:45, I Corinthians 15:47, I John 2:2, Romans 3:28, Psalms 25, Psalms 102:17.
Discussion Question Scriptures: Romans 3:25, Exodus 25:21, Psalms 25:10 & 18, Psalms 102:17, II Corinthians 3:3.

# Chapter 12 ~ Thursday

# I cry out to you Lord

P op! Crack! Rumble! The sky shouted with thunder as the lightning flashed, filling the Cabin in the Deep Dark Woods with a brilliant showing of light. Then for an instant, while the thunder shook that old one-room schoolhouse, it seemed for a moment that it was going to be shaken from its foundation. Marcus thought, "It wasn't supposed to rain today!" After that, a hard downpour ensued as the sun was almost ready to break on the horizon. Marcus was afraid that this storm was going to delay the project. Andrea thought, "Coffee time with my new hubby." The young woman sprang out of bed and darted into the kitchen, starting the coffee maker. "We might as well have a hot cup of coffee together since you're not going to be working this morning," Andrea said. Marcus reluctantly agreed as he was not a big fan of working in the lightning.

Over at the ranger station where the crew members stayed, the thunder and lightning also paid an early morning visit. Jeff opened his eyes as another blinding flash turned the early morning darkness to light. CRACK went another round of thunder and lightning, waking up everyone at the ranger station. Being the first one up, Claire began to make her tea as Cliff and Jeff preferred coffee. While the rain was falling, everyone at the ranger station had their morning brew of choice. Soon they all gathered around the table. Then Claire reluctantly placed her hand on Jeff's arm and announced to him, "Honey, yesterday afternoon, I repented of my sins and accepted Jesus Christ as my personal savior at the pavilion with Lucas and Andrea." Noah gave her a cheer with his coffee cup. Jacob said, "Praise the Lord in heaven; that's wonderful news, Claire. I'm very happy for you." However, her very own husband questioned her about her newly acquired faith. Jeff demanded: "So, Claire, did you confess all your sins to Jesus?! Or did you keep the really big ones to yourself?! Do you even know what sin is?! I mean, every time I read the Bible, it says, sin is this and sin is that, but I have never found a good description of what sin really is! So, what could you possibly confess if you can't tell me what sin is?! Claire! What exactly is sin?!" Claire was speechless as she looked into the eyes of her very own husband, seeing a depth of hatred that she knew existed, but one she had refused to acknowledge until now.

As another round of thunder and lightning flashed its way across the heavens. The sun began to rise, taking command of the sky above the clouds and storm. Jacob spoke up, saying to Jeff: "You see, Jeff, sin is nothing to play around with. A sin is a thought, action, or encounter that inhibits one's mind from believing that they have a right to dwell in the holiness of God. In other words, sin is the result of a choice that brings about a guilty conscience. She has acknowledged that it was Jesus Christ who took the sin of the world upon himself (John 1:29). In accepting Jesus as her savior, Claire acknowledged that the blood of Jesus was shed on the cross for the remission of her sin" (Matthew 26:28). Jeff, being a little more cordial as he spoke to Jacob, said, "Well, that's great, but you still haven't told me what sin is." Jacob happened to have his Bible with him at the table, and he said, "Jeff, I'm going to read to you from James 4:17 'Therefore, to him who knows to do good and does not do it, to him it is sin.' Now I'm going to read from I John 3:4, which says, 'Whoever commits sin also commits lawlessness, and sin is lawlessness.'"

Cliff gave his thought on sin, "I know when I sin because I feel the guilt of it right away. I just can't give a good definition of sin."

Then Claire spoke up and said, "Sin is a feeling in your own heart that you have done something wrong against someone or against God." Noah said, "When you're sitting in your prison cell, you have to become honest with your own heart and acknowledge your sin before God because it just begins to eat you up." "That's right, Noah," Jacob said. Jeff interrupted him and said, "I don't feel any sin or any guilt of sin—I haven't committed a crime or anything like that." Jeff just rolled his eyes as Jacob turned his Bible to Galatians 3:22 and read: "But the Scriptures declare that we are all prisoners of sin, so we receive God's promise of freedom only by believing in Jesus Christ" [NLT]. Then Claire said, "I believe Jesus died for my sins, and I acknowledge Him as my savior." At that, Jeff got up from the table. As he did, his chair fell over backward. He bent over in a fit of rage and picked it up, slamming it to the ground. Then walking away, he was mumbling curse words under his breath while flinging his arms into the air. All the while, Jim was lying on his cot, thinking about that Sunday morning when he was a kid. It was the day when one of the youth leaders from his church asked all of the students, "Does anyone want to be saved today?" Almost all of the children in the room responded by standing up and reciting the sinners' prayer. As Jim was only a kid then, he began to question if that day so long ago had any merit, or was it just a kid thing?

While Marcus and Andrea were finishing up their coffee and breakfast, Lucas sped by the front of the cabin, splashing the mud as he went by. Andrea just rolled her eyes as her smile quickly turned to laughter. Then, Lucas walked into the cabin and said, "I knew this storm wasn't going to last very long." After a few minutes of small talk, Lucas and Marcus speed off in the John Deere to start another workday.

The crew had assembled for the morning safety briefing. Marcus said to them, "This morning, we're going to be removing the iron gate from the adit with the welder." Soon enough, they were all hard at work, losing only a couple of hours to the storm.

Jim and Steve held the iron gate from falling while Katie-Bird began cutting away the iron bars that secured it to the side of the mountain. Keith was working on a few minor repairs on the locomotive. Noah was working on wheel number nine. Jim and Cliff were busy laying out the train track securing it to the wooden runners with the iron spikes. Jacob had taken an interest in helping with laying the track. He brought over another wooden runner. Cliff took advantage of the situation and asked him a few questions. Cliff was still not sure about the power of sin. So, Jacob began to explain faith to him by saying: **"You see Cliff, it was God the Father who raised Jesus from the dead. Jesus died because of our offenses rising the third day, for our justification, forgiving us of our sin before God. This is what we as Christians believe when we say that we have been saved." ([5] Romans 4:23-25).** Jeff heard what Jacob said, but he chose to ignore it. His heart was hardened to the thought of the saving grace of Jesus. Marcus also listened to what Jacob had to say about justification and sin. Still, he, too, didn't want to be bothered with religion.

As Andrea was hiking alone, she stopped at the miners' village. She was once again thinking about the dream of Jason and the news journal reading of Katie as she began to pray over her future children.

"Dear Heavenly Father, I cry out to You, Lord, on behalf of my son and daughter. When they are born, create in them a new heart, oh God. Let them experience Your power and Your presence throughout their lifetime. Father God, break any strongholds that come over their lives that the enemy has launched their way. Cancel any assignments from the evil one concerning my future children. Rescue them from a life of sin. Break every yoke of bondage that would ensnare them. Please turn their hearts, minds, and actions towards You, Jesus. Give them a hungering and a thirsting for Your word in their personal life. Deepen their understanding of who You are, Oh, Lord. I pray for a fresh outpouring of Your Spirit upon them on the day that they are born. Please remove each and every evil influence, relationship, and friendship that comes into their lives. Replace those ungodly influences with healthy and Godly relationships. Please, Father, do a mighty work in and through my precious children. Place a guard over their mouth, and teach them what they should say. Guard their hearts, minds, and spirit. Let the conviction of the Holy Spirit come upon them early in their lives and rescue them from the enemy's ploy. This I ask in the name of Jesus. Amen."

Claire was on a hike and happened by the miners' village just as Andrea had finished her prayer. Andrea was still visibly shaken from her deep prayer when Claire walked up to her and asked, "Andrea, is everything alright?" "Yes, I was just praying for my children," Andrea answered. "Oh, I didn't know you and Marcus had any children," Claire said. Andrea opened up to Claire about the dreams and the news journal articles. Then Claire opened up to Andrea about how hateful her husband had acted that morning when she told him she had accepted Jesus as her savior. Claire was expecting Andrea to say something like, you don't need him anymore, or he sure is a jerk. But instead, Andrea asked Claire, "Would you like to pray for Jeff right now?" "Sure," Claire said, pausing for a moment, and then she said, "Dear heavenly Father... Claire went into great detail about her petition for her husband's salvation. She even reminded God that Jeff was brought up in a Godly home at the end of her prayer. Andrea thought, "Wow, she really loves that man."

Before long at the mine, Cliff, Jeff, Jacob, Lucas, and Marcus were laying down the track for the mine railway system. They were going like a machine, having laid down 200 feet of the track before lunch. The last 150' was to go inside the mine. That left only 150' to lay down that afternoon, and Marcus was ecstatic. Noah was working on wheel number ten, and Keith was replacing the last of the old steam hoses on the locomotive. Noah said, "That sure looks like a new piece of equipment you got there." "I think this little pup is going to be a great addition to this park," Keith said. He was referring to when the mine was cleared out, the Edwardsville Ranger Station would be opened to the public. They would be advertising miniature steam engine train rides. This was the main reason that the parks department received that grant money in the first place. The mine carts would be displayed at the ranger station's historical display. The steam mine locomotive was going to be the big draw. It would provide rides to the public on new passenger cars used to tour the historic mine, eventually extending to other parts of the property.

Another aspect of this project, the shoring operation, began later that afternoon. That was needed to ensure the mine would not sustain any further collapses, protecting the crew during the removal of the time capsule and the public during tours of the old mine. A section at the end of the mine was large enough to make a complete turnaround where a switching platform would be located. The train would make a wide curve to the right, then loop around, triggering the switch that would allow the train to merge back onto the track, touring the mine in the forward direction at all times.

As the crew was breaking for lunch, Cliff asked Jacob, "What does it mean to be justified by the blood of Jesus?" "That's a great question, Cliff," Jacob said, giving him this answer:

"To understand justification, we must first look at faith, and faith is the reliance on Christ for our salvation. Therefore, justification is simply that we are rendered innocent of our sin, thus giving us peace with God through our Lord Jesus Christ. Now, Cliff, one essential item to remember is that we have access by faith into this grace. This grace that Jesus has extended to us is an influence upon our lives through the Holy Spirit. This gives us the ability to live pleasing to God, rejoicing in our praise and worship. Cliff, I want to be clear that we can't expect God to honor our praise and worship if we are only thankful in our times of plenty; we have to also thank God in our times of suffering. What I mean is this, when we are burdened down with hardships or sicknesses, we must understand that these troubles that we have to work through are to accomplish patience and endurance. These tribulations that we go through in life, such as losing a job or, even worse, losing a loved one, work to accomplish our endurance. This endurance gives us proof of faith and hope, which is essentially confidence. This confidence that we have in our life makes us not ashamed of the love that God has poured out in our hearts by the Holy Spirit, whom we have received. ([6] Romans 5:1-5).

Oh, there is one more thing that I must mention, and that is the blood. The blood of Jesus was poured out for you and me, enabling us to be forgiven of our sins. I should be clear; our sins are our offenses to men or to God or both. But the main point that I should make to you is that the New Testament is more than just a series of books. It is also a covenant that Jesus has made available to all who believe in Him" (Matthew 26:28 [KJV]).

Jim just listened to Jacob taking in everything that the older gentleman had to say to Cliff. Marcus also heard the older man's speech, but he pushed those words to the back of his mind. Just like the time capsule had been left in that mine for so many years. But who would clear out Marcus's mind and bring all these thoughts of God into action?

As Andrea and Claire continued their hike, they came across the Edwardsville boathouse. Entering in, they met one of the rangers who had prepared a boat for them. "Here's the oars," Ranger Bruce said as he handed one to Andrea and the other one to Claire. Andrea busted out in laughter when she saw the look on Clair's face. Claire said, "A rowboat! We're going out on the lake in a rowboat!?"

**Discussion Questions:**
1) In this chapter, Clair announced to everyone that she had accepted Jesus as her savior the day before. What do you think about her husband's response?
2) What would you have said if you could chime in on the group's discussion on sin at the ranger station in this chapter?
3) After reading Andrea's prayer over her future children's lives, what would you say to God about your children? You could

use the prayer from this chapter that Andrea said over your own children if you can't find any words of your own.

Note: Andrea's prayer in this chapter about her future children is an actual prayer that a woman spoke over her own child.

Scriptures: John 1:29, Matthew 26:28, James 4:17, I John 3:4, Galatians 3:22, Romans 4:23-25, Romans 5:1-5, Matthew 26:28.

Discussion Question Scriptures: none.

# Chapter 13 ~ Thursday

# The Throne of Grace

With the iron gate removed, the crew concentrated their efforts on shoring up the opening to the mine. Jim, Steve, and Katie-Bird began the task of assembling the heavy wooden timbers forming them into beams and posts across the adit—the entrance to the mine. The three of them worked diligently as they had also been tasked with mounting the new doors that would be used to secure the mine entrance.

As Andrea rowed the boat out on the lake, Claire was surprised at the beauty of the scenery. Clair said, "Andrea, it is just breathtaking out here." The two women continued rowing as they approached an area along the Islands' shoreline where some cypress stumps, cattails, and lily pads were. Andrea rowed the boat closer to the island. Claire said, "I don't understand why people persist in littering." Then she reached down and pulled an old bottle out of the water, tossing it into the boat. Andrea said, "This rowing thing is harder than I expected." She was steering the rowboat towards the island so they could do some exploring.

As Claire jumped out of the boat, she pulled it up onto the beach, tying the rope to a piece of driftwood that was partially buried in the sand. Andrea laid aside the oars and stepped to the front, kicking the bottle that Claire had thrown into the boat earlier. "Claire, did you notice that there was a note inside this bottle?" Andrea asked her as she picked it up. "Let me see that," Claire said. Andrea handed her the bottle while stepping out of the boat. Pulling the cork out, Claire turned it over, and a note fell out into her hand. And there, across the top of the note, were the words: *The Way News Journal.* Claire began to read aloud:

*My Dearest, Andrea, and Claire have faith in God and know that your prayers have been received, having been spoken before the throne of grace. You have a great High Priest who has passed through the heavens, Jesus the Son of God. You must hold fast to the acknowledgment of your faith. You have a High Priest who can sympathize with your situations. He was tempted just as you both have been, yet without sin. As you have come boldly to the throne of grace in prayer, be faithful that you will obtain mercy and find grace to help in your time of need (Hebrews 4:14-16).*

Claire put the cork back in the bottle and tossed it back into the boat. Then the two women started exploring the island. They continued to look over this latest news journal as they walked along. There was also a man wearing a hooded cloak on the island as the two women explored.

Back at the mine: The new security doors had been installed. Noah was reconditioning work cart wheel number eleven. Keith was polishing the new brass bell on the front of his little locomotive. He had completed most of his other projects. Jim, Steve, and Katie-Bird were finished with their shoring operation for that day. The rest of the crew was busy laying down the miniature rail track. The project would be moving inside the mine the next day, where the remainder of the miniature track was to be laid. Lucas and Jacob were nailing the track pieces to the runners. Jacob said to Lucas, "Claire told me that she accepted Jesus Christ as her savior at the pavilion yesterday."

Cliff and Jim began to assist Jacob and Lucas with nailing the track to the wooden runners while Marcus supervised. Lucas said, "Yes, Claire didn't hesitate for a moment. She knew that she needed to have a personal relationship with Jesus. It was as if Isaiah 57:15 flashed right before my eyes." Jacob said, "I know it well. ...I dwell in the high and holy place, With him who has a contrite and humble spirit…" Lucas said, "That's better than I could have done. I saw it yesterday with my own eyes." While the two men talked, Jim asked Jacob about his Sunday school sinners' prayer dilemma because his heart had been troubled with all the talk lately about Jesus and sin. As he did, Cliff also perked up and listened. Jacob responded to his question by saying:

"Jim, I have had people ask me this same question many times. It really is valid and one I enjoy speaking about. We must understand with our heart that Jesus died for the ungodly. Jim, can you think of anyone that would be willing to lay down their life for you? The answer is Jesus. Jesus demonstrated His love for us by dying on the cross while we were still sinners. It is the blood of Jesus that makes us innocent, freeing us from the wrath of God, thus making us whole. Before we believed in the name of Jesus, we were considered by God enemies of Jesus. Having accepted the saving grace of Jesus, we are reconciled, being saved by His life. So, we are full of joy, having been reconciled to God by Jesus Christ. ([7] Romans 5:6-11).

So, back to your question, you stood up and said a sinner's prayer. Keep in mind that when Jesus told the woman her sins were forgiven in Luke 7:36-50, she never spoke a word in that passage. Jesus knew her heart just as He knows your heart. It's not so important what you said that day when you were a child; what is important is what your heart said to God."

Those words also set a mark on Cliff's heart resting in that tender place when he was a kid in Sunday school. Marcus also felt those words somewhere in his own heart.

At the conclusion of their boating excursion, the two ladies approached the dock. Claire said, "I'm going to be sore tomorrow. I can't believe how hard it was to row this boat." Andrea just smiled as she tied the rowboat to the dock. After stepping onto the dock, Andrea extended her hand out to Claire and helped her out of the boat. "Did you two ladies have a nice time?" Ranger Bruce asked while he untied the rowboat from the dock cleat. "That was hard work rowing that little boat. We had to switch off just to make it back," Andrea said as the two women were walking to the boathouse. "Hey, ladies, don't forget your trash," Ranger Bruce said. Then he pulled the rowboat onto the dock for storage. "Oh, sorry," Claire said as she walked back and took the bottle out that they had left in the boat. She tucked that old bottle under her arm as she carried the life jackets in her other arm. Andrea said to Claire, "I'll follow you back to the boathouse with the oars."

Soon, Andrea and Claire were hiking along the fourth marked trail. Andrea noticed that Claire was still holding the bottle. She said to Claire, "You forgot to put that old bottle in the trash before we left the boathouse." Claire held the bottle out in front of her, being surprised that she still had it. Looking at Andrea, Claire said, "There's another note in it." Then she turned the bottle over and pulled the cork out, and the note fell to the ground. Andrea picked it up and read:

*The Way News Journal*
*Isaiah 57:15-21*

"What does that mean?" Claire asked as she eagerly grabbed the news journal from Andrea. Andrea shrugged her shoulders and said, "Do you want to go back to the cabin with me? It looks like we're going to have to look this one up."

Back at the mine, all the men struggled as they had to manually lift the mine steam locomotive onto the track. They had just finished the last 150' of track that was to go outside the mine. Next, they moved the first work cart with its newly reconditioned wheels onto the track hooking it up to the locomotive. "We might as well hook up the second work cart," Cliff said because it was also ready. Noah was finishing with wheel number eleven and said, "I'm just going to weld this one on before I finish today." Then Marcus gave an end of day briefing by saying:

> "We all made a lot of progress today because of your work hard. Tomorrow we will be utilizing the locomotive and the three work carts to begin the process of removing the debris from the mine and

shoring up the drift as we go. We will be backing the mine train into the drift, loading it with the rocks. Then we will dump the debris from the work carts, where we cleared out the rock pile earlier this week. We will lay the remainder of the track inside the mine as we go throughout the day. Noah said that he would have the last cart wheel welded back on to work cart number three in the morning. I'll see you all back here first thing tomorrow; that is as long as it doesn't storm again."

Later that evening, Andrea and Marcus were having dinner alone. They began to discuss their future children and the values they would need to establish in their home. Andrea said, "Marcus, God has placed on my heart that we will need to raise our children in a godly environment." Marcus said, "I couldn't agree with you more." However, he still concealed a secret that would prevent him from providing any godly influence in his home.

Later that night, while Andrea was fast asleep, worn out from her row boating excursion, Marcus came across her open Bible laying on the kitchen table. He picked it up and read from the news journal marking the passage that she and Claire had read that afternoon.

*The Way News Journal*
*Isaiah 57:15-21*

**Discussion Questions:**

1) From Hebrews 4:14-16, do you understand that Jesus was tempted the same as you are? Are you willing to come before the throne of grace in your time of need and cry out to Jesus in prayer?

2) From Isaiah 57:15, do you understand that Jesus recognizes the humble and the contrite person? If you were to approach the throne of grace in humility, what would God's response be?

3) In Luke 7:36-50, Jesus forgave a woman of her sins and then said to her, "Your faith has saved you. Go in peace." This woman never spoke a word, and yet she became saved. As you read this passage, what are some of the key elements that Jesus

would have noticed that led to His announcement in verse 48, "Your sins are forgiven?"

Scriptures: Hebrews 4:14-16, Isaiah 57:15, Romans 5:6-11, Luke 7:36-50, Isaiah 57:15-21.

Discussion Question Scriptures: Hebrews 4:14-16, Isaiah 57:15, Luke 7:36-50.

# Chapter 14 ~ Friday

# Like the Troubled Sea

Jeff was the first one to wake up at the ranger station. As he got out of bed, he found an open Bible lying on the bed where Clair was still sleeping. It had *The Way News Journal* from Hebrews 4:14-16, marking that passage. Taking her Bible with him, Jeff made his way to the table and began reading the passage from Hebrews. Picking up the news journal that Claire found in the bottle out on the lake, he read over it several times. Then he began to question within himself, "Could I be the reason that Claire was praying about in her time of need?" Jeff started to meditate on the words from the passage of scripture and *The Way News Journal*. However, he knew in his heart what Claire's time of need meant to her.

Looking at the clock, he noticed it was only 2:37 AM. Jeff asked himself, "Why do I persist in hurting a good woman?" He knew that he was the subject of her prayers and also her grief. "I was pretty hard on her yesterday morning," he thought as a feeling of shame came flowing over him. "Why have I become the kind of man who must despise his own wife? Why can't I lift her up just once in her life?" Jeff asked himself that question once more, but this time he was digging deeper into his heart. Deep down, he truly loved his wife; however, his heart was still hard. Jeff knew that he wasn't going back to sleep anytime soon, so he began thumbing through her Bible as he had nothing better to do at that time of the morning.

Over at the cabin, Marcus woke up before his alarm. It was 5:19 AM, and he could no longer lay in bed. Having left Andrea's Bible on the kitchen table the night before, he began to read from Isaiah 57:15-21 once again. There were some words in that passage that seemed to pierce his heart. Was this the beginning of a crack on his hard shell of a heart that he felt piercing his spirit while reading the Bible?

> Isaiah 57:20 But the wicked are like the troubled sea, When it cannot rest, Whose waters cast up mire and dirt. 21 "There is no peace," Says my God, "for the wicked."

He read it again and again. He could hear those words speaking a message to his heart that became louder every time. Marcus thought, "What could this mean?" He already knew the answer in the deep part of his heart, mind, and spirit. Then Marcus heard a small knock at the door. He looked up from the kitchen table, seeing the first ray of sunshine beaming through the treetops and the fog shining into the cabin. It was nature's way of saying good morning. Lucas knocked a little harder, then Marcus realized that it was time to go to work.

The crew was prompt as they had assembled at the mine entrance for the morning briefing. Marcus went over the planned events for the day. The crew was beaming with pride as they all had worked tirelessly to meet the original goal. The assignments were given out, and everyone was hard at work once again.

Cliff saw one of the cart wheels lying on the workbench. Then he said, "Noah, did you forget about this cart wheel?" Noah replied, "Thanks, that was the one that Marcus worked on the other day. He forgot to give it back to me." Picking up the last wheel, Cliff handed it to Noah, and he began to weld it back onto the cart. After Noah finished welding the last wheel, Jacob said, "Way to go, little cuz, that looks like wheel number twelve to me." Then he said to the others, "Hey guys, let's get this last work cart on the track." The four of the men picked up the work cart and loaded it onto the track connecting it to the other two work carts. Lucas said, "That sure looks great, I can't believe we pulled it off, but you guys came together as a team and got this little steam train restored and back on the tracks." So, the crew began firing up the steam engine, and soon it was hot enough to transfer power to the drive wheels. Keith started backing the train into the mine.

Jim, Steve, and Katie-Bird were setting the beams and posts, shoring the mind drift. Marcus said, "This sure is a coordinated effort." Lucas went over the roster assignments with Marcus for the remainder of the crew. He said, "Jacob, Noah, Cliff, and Jeff are loading the rocks and debris into the work carts. I have Claire working as a safety spotter as Keith backs the train into the mine." Marcus was once again ecstatic as the project was moving in what he called—the positive direction. Marcus exclaimed, "We're going to meet our goal!" Marcus took the opportunity to check the mine layout plans and ensure that everything was according to the drawings. Keith backed the mine train into the mine so the first load of rocks could be hauled out. Cliff noticed that Jeff wasn't acting like his usual self and said to him, "Jeff, you don't seem to be yourself today."

While still at the cabin, Andrea had decided to hike down to the mine and see the crew's progress. She was especially excited to see the mine train in action. Marcus had told her the night before that it would be up and running first thing in the morning. Before she left the cabin, she noticed another news journal on the table in-between the two rocking chairs. She looked at her coffee and said to herself, "I better drink this one fast before it gets cold." Sitting down in the rocking chair, she picked up the next edition of *The Way News Journal* and began to read:

*Andrea, God spoke to me shortly after the creation and told me that I may eat the fruit of the trees in the garden. But He also warned me that I was not to eat from the tree of the knowledge of good and evil next to the beautiful one because I would certainly die if I ate from it. I was also not permitted to touch it. And I had even been warned by God to never look at that tree. This, God was firm on.*

*Yours truly ~ Eve*

*My dearest Andrea, I regret to inform you that Eve could not resist the serpent's words, and she ate the fruit of the tree of the knowledge of good and evil. Then she gave the fruit to her husband Adam, and he also ate of it. I had spent countless hours going over the dangers of temptation with both of them. In the end, the devious words of the serpent tricked her. Andrea, you will be faced with your own temptations. You must be strong as the devil desires to sift you like wheat with his lies. As I told Eve in the garden, don't look at the tree of the knowledge of good and evil, don't touch it, and don't eat from it. However, on the day the serpent came to her, she could not resist his lies. It came down to this: he tricked her into taking her eyes off of Me. Everyone falls to some degree or another when they take their eyes off of Me. Even Peter looked away on the troubled sea. He also denied me three times one night, even denying his discipleship. (Genesis 2:8-25 & 3:1-24, Luke 4:8, John 18:15-18 & 18:25-27, Luke 22:31, and Matthew 14:29-33).*

*The key to overcoming temptation is to follow the example that I have set for you. When temptation comes your way, follow My example. This is what I said to the serpent in Luke 4:8, "Get behind Me, Satan! For it is written,' You shall worship the LORD your God, and Him only you shall serve.'"*
*Your Lord and Savior*
*Jesus*

As Andrea finished reading the news journal, she reached for her coffee, and once again, she found it to be cold. She was getting used to reading these news journals, but she was uncertain about what this one meant. She asked herself, "What am I going to be tempted with, and when will this happen?"

Back at the mine, Noah said, "This is sure backbreaking work." "Little cuz, there are only 95 feet to go until we reach that time capsule," Jacob said as he began to laugh. "That should do it," Cliff said as the three work carts were full and needed to be dumped. Keith drove the steam locomotive out of the mine with the first load of debris to the dumpsite. The style of work carts that the mining company had used was the side dumping model. When Keith arrived at the dumpsite, he pulled the dump lever allowing the first work cart to tip to the side, dumping the rocks into a pile. Keith did this with the other two work carts, also dumping their loads to the side.

While Keith was dumping the first load of debris, Cliff asked Jacob another question about sin. He asked, "I just don't understand why the Bible says that everyone is a sinner." Jacob said: "Cliff, what you must understand is that sin entered the world through Adam, and the result of that sin was death to all of his descendants. All people will die because of that one man's sin, which resulted in a judgment of death. However, through the grace of Jesus Christ, he offered the free gift of the Holy Spirit, which resulted in justification. In other words, Adam was disobedient to God, resulting in all his descendants being sinners. Then Jesus Christ being obedient to His Father's will, resulted in many being made righteous." ([8] Romans 5:12-21).

Claire yelled, "Guys, the train is coming." As Keith backed the train into the mine, he rang the shiny brass bell, warning everyone that he was coming. Then the crew went back to work again, removing the debris from the drift. Cliff looked at Jacob and said, "It seems I have found a gold nugget amongst these rocks." He was referring to Jacob's lessons from the book of Romans.

The shoring operation was going well, and they were 25 feet into the mine, having already cleared the debris out to that point. Andrea arrived at the worksite and noticed that the old iron gate had been removed. Marcus walked up to her and said, "Would you like to see the progress that we have made?" The two of them walked into the mine and saw Jeff and Claire having a discussion. Then Jeff looked over at Andrea and said, "I want to thank you for giving Claire your Bible." Andrea said, "I never gave Claire a Bible." Claire said to Jeff, "Jacob gave me that Bible." Marcus wasn't interested in the Bible discussion until Jeff said he found a news journal article in the Bible she got from Jacob. Marcus asked him, "Jeff, have you seen one also?" Jeff responded: "Not only have I seen one, but I feel something every time I read it. Just this morning, I read a passage that Claire prayed over me, and I must say I was more than touched. I haven't been that good to her through the years, and I don't know why she still loves me, but after reading that news journal this morning, I have decided to become a better husband." With that, the tears began to flow down Claire's face as she looked into the eyes of her husband, knowing in her heart that for the first time in many years, he was sincere.

Jacob couldn't help overhearing their discussion as he remembered the passage from Psalms 107 that he read to Clair when he gave her his Bible the morning of the storm:

> [27]They reel to and fro, and stagger like a drunken man, And are at their wits' end. [28]Then they cry out to the LORD in their trouble, And He brings them out of their distresses. [29]He calms the storm, So that its waves are still.

**Discussion Questions:**

1) In this chapter, Jeff asked himself, "Why do I persist in hurting a good woman?" Shortly before Jeff asked himself that question, Claire prayed from her heart in brokenness of spirit that the Lord would touch him with the Holy Spirit. Which are you? The one who is praying to God for a loved one? Or the one whom a loved one is praying to God for?

2) "There is no peace for the wicked." This is a quote from God—Isaiah 57:21. Who are the wicked ones? To address this question, seek guidance from Galatians 5:16-26.

3) From Romans 3:23, who does the Bible say has sinned? Answer: All have sinned…
Further, read Ecclesiastes 7:20, For there is not a just man on earth who does good And does not sin.

4) In this chapter, Cliff asked Jacob, "Why does the Bible say that everyone is a sinner." What is the remedy to sin?
Answer: From Romans 3:25-26, [vs. 25] Remember from an earlier News Journal article (Chapter 11), propitiation was a covering by His blood, and [vs. 26] that He might be the justifier of the one who has faith in Jesus. So, through faith, one is saved by the blood, thus making them justified and clear of sin in the eyes of God. Therefore the answer to (What is the remedy to sin?) is repentance and faith by the blood of Jesus.

Scriptures: Hebrews 4:14-16, Isaiah 57:15-21, Genesis 2:8-25 & 3:1-24, Luke 4:8, John 18:15-18, John 18:25-27, Luke 22:31, Matthew 14:29-33, Romans 5:12-21, Psalms 107:27-29.
Discussion Question Scriptures: Isaiah 57:21, Galatians 5:16-26, Romans 3:23, Ecclesiastes 7:20, Romans 3:25-26.

# Chapter 15 ~ Friday

# A Prayer That Still Moves the Heart of God

Claire said, "I'm sure glad I came with you. I've seen enough of that mine for one day." Then she added, "This place is freaky." "WATCH OUT!" Andrea yelled. As Claire walked, she almost hit her head on an old rusty nail sticking out of a board. Andrea said, "Bless his heart, Lucas thinks this is the coolest place on the property." The two women were touring the old office building and dormitory that had fallen down during a blizzard that hit Edwardsville many years ago. "I'm just not feeling it," Claire said. Andrea agreed, "Me neither." Then she asked, "What do you say we go back to the ranger station and take advantage of their free coffee and tea?" Claire said, "That's the best idea I've heard all day."

Soon, Claire and Andrea were at the ranger station with their hot drinks in hand. As they walked into the classroom, they noticed a plaque that said:

> In honor of the late Pastor Daniel Edwards, for which
> the town was named.

Andrea said, "I didn't know that," Claire said. "That's pretty cool to know who this town was named after." "Oh look, there's a prayer under Daniel Edwards' plaque," Andrea said. As the two women stood there reading the prayer, they felt a weighty presence in the room, like the Spirit of God. Andrea said, "Reading this prayer gives me the goosebumps." "Hey, there's more over here," Claire said, as she pointed to another plaque under the prayer that said:

> This was the prayer of a man named Daniel Edwards, who had a deep conviction to the will of God. He prayed this prayer before he started to build his church. It is the cabin located on the other side of Edwardsville. Pastor Edwards had intended to call it the Church in the Way, signifying the way of the saints (Acts 9:1-2). The name stuck, thus becoming what it is today: The Cabin in the Way. It has been said that this man's prayer made its way to the throne of grace (Hebrews 4:16).

"Wow, that's something to think about," Claire said. Andrea looked puzzled. Then Claire said, "The way—you know—the way news journals that you have been reading." The wheels began spinning in Andrea's head. Then something clicked into place, and she sat her yellow hiking hat on the table, under the plaque. Then she asked, "Could it be possible that a man so many years ago prayed a prayer that still moves the heart of God today?" Claire said, "Well, that would explain how Jeff found a news journal article of the prayer I prayed over him. How else could he have known that I even prayed for him?"

Back at the mine: "I will sure be glad when all this track is laid," Jeff said while he and Cliff kept pace with the shoring operation and the debris removal. They were laying the track down inside the mine. Jeff asked Cliff as they were nailing the rail-track pieces to the runners, "What have you and Jacob been talking about while you work?" Cliff answered: "Haven't you felt a sense of peace while working around Jacob? I've been asking him questions ever since Claire said she accepted Jesus as her Savior. I want to know what sin is and what I'm supposed to do about it in my own life. There's more to life than working and getting drunk at the end of the day. I haven't had a drink since that storm hit the other morning. This place is really shaking me up. I almost don't know what to think, but somehow deep down, I know the answer." The two of them worked in silence until they heard that familiar sound of Keith ringing the brass bell while he backed the train into the mine for another load of debris. Jeff began to think about the discussions that had taken place about sin, the news journal articles, and the Bible that Jacob had given to Claire. Then he said under his breath, "This place is really shaking me up too, Cliff."

Marcus arrived back at the mine from the ranger station and yelled to Lucas, "Follow me!" The two men walked out of the mine at a fast pace. Lucas could hardly keep up as he wondered what Marcus was up to. Marcus said, "Lucas, I was reviewing the mine plans earlier, and I found a notation in the legend for a light switch. I disregarded it at first, that was until I remembered the overhead lights in the mine." Before that day, the crew had only seen the inside of the mine from the plans stored at the ranger station. Marcus asked Lucas, "Do you know of any switches that may be nearby that could turn on the overhead lights in the mine?" "Follow me!" Lucas said as he also tore off at a fast pace with Marcus right behind him. Lucas walked over to a power pole and pushed a tree branch out of the way. Then he said to Marcus, "Is this what you're looking for?" Marcus put his hand on the electrical junction box and turned the switch to the on position. Then, at that exact moment, a loud cheer was heard coming from the mine as the lights came on, chasing the darkness away.

The lights illuminated the mine as Keith hauled out another load of debris. "Aren't you tired yet, Jacob?" Cliff asked. The older gentleman bent over to pick up something that fell out of his shirt pocket. "I'm getting pretty tired, but we got to get this job done," Jacob said. "What have you got there?" Cliff asked as Jacob tucked something back into his pocket. "This is my New Testament Bible. I always carry it with me," Jacob said. Lucas yelled into the mine, "It's lunchtime boys, come on out here and dig in," "Now I know how the minors must've felt," Jeff said, as everyone was making their way for some chow and a needed break.

Jeff said to Jacob as they were walking out of the mine, "I want to thank you for giving Claire your Bible and the news journal. It really means a lot to us." Jacob said, "I gave her that Bible all right, but I don't know anything about a news journal." Jeff said, "You know—*The Way News Journal*—that had an article from Hebrews and a prayer that Claire prayed over me." "No, I don't know anything about that. I just gave her my Bible," Jacob said. Jeff was a little confused as he thought that Jacob had something to do with *The Way News Journal* that he found in Claire's Bible. Jeff asked, "Jacob, can you tell me what I am supposed to do about the sin in my life." Cliff smiled as he had just discussed that same topic with Jacob earlier.

> Jacob said: "Jeff, it is our man of sin, our sin nature, that needs to be crucified with Jesus so that our sin can be done away with. This is the only way that we will no longer desire to serve sin. When we die to sin, we become free from it. In dying to sin, we believe that we will live with Christ. We know that once Christ was raised from the dead, He would never die again. Death no longer had authority over Him. When He died on the cross, He died for sin once and for all. Now he lives to do the will of His Father. ([9] Romans 6:6-10). The only thing that you can do about sin is to repent of it. Without repentance, there is no remission of sins (Luke 24:44-49). Jesus had a message about repentance in Mark 1:15, where He said, 'The time is fulfilled, and the kingdom of God is at hand. Repent, and believe in the gospel.'"

After that explanation from Jacob, the hungry workers arrived at the picnic table and dove into the pizza boxes. Jeff said to Cliff, "Do you want meat lovers or cheese." "I'll take a piece of cheese," Cliff answered. Handing Cliff his piece of pizza, Jeff said to him, "Are you okay? You seem a little down in the dumps today." Then Cliff turned to Jacob and said, "Before Thursday, I hadn't given any thought to sin, but now I feel it welling up in the pit of my stomach as if I could just vomit it up." Jacob responded, "Cliff, what you are feeling is godly sorrow." Jacob took his New Testament Bible out of his shirt pocket. He opened it to II Corinthians chapter 7, slowly turning the pages. Cliff was in eager anticipation of what the older gentleman would say. All the while, he held his piece of pizza in his hand, forgetting his hunger for the moment.

Jacob said: "That feeling in the pit of your stomach is godly sorrow. It is godly sorrow that leads to repentance. Your sins are being stirred up in your heart. What you are going through is—you are rejecting your sins of the past. This godly sorrow is the place in your life when you begin to reject your sins and begin to embrace the truth in Jesus Christ. By casting off your sins in repentance, you embrace the righteousness of Jesus Christ. Now, Cliff, you need to embrace the repentance that God is granting you." After that latest explanation from Jacob, Cliff said, "I just don't know what to do." Jacob said, "Cliff, somehow deep down, I think you know the answer."

Then with his piece of pizza still in hand, the tears began streaming down Cliff's face. He said: "Dear Jesus, hear my prayer as I have many regrets in my life. All I ask is that You have mercy upon me, O God, according to Your lovingkindness. According to the multitude of Your tender mercies, blot out my transgressions. Wash me thoroughly from my iniquity, and cleanse me from my sin. For I acknowledge my transgressions, and my sin is always before me. Against You, You only, have I sinned, and done this evil in Your sight." After that, Cliff broke out in a deep sob as he had just poured out all the regrets of his heart, having acknowledged his sin nature and rejected it through true and sincere repentance that only comes from the heart. (Psalms 51:1-4, II Corinthians 7:8-12, II Timothy 2:25-26).

Ranger Bruce yelled, "Andrea," while he ran after the two women at the ranger station. He was trying to catch them while they were walking out the door. "Andrea, here's your mail; it just came today," Ranger Bruce said after he finally caught up to them.

Opening the envelope, Andrea read those words again, *The Way News Journal.*

*My dearest Andrea, you must know and comprehend the meaning of the Tree of Life, the Beautiful One, that you saw in My garden as you walked with Me. But first, I want to warn you that you are not to labor for the food that perishes. Instead, you are to labor for the food which endures to everlasting life, which I will give to you because My Father has set His seal upon Me. I am the living bread of God who came down from heaven, and I gave My life for the world. I am the bread of life. He who comes to Me will never be hungry, and he who believes in Me will never thirst. All the people that My Father gives to Me will come to Me. Everyone who comes to me I will not reject. I came down from heaven not to do My will but to do the will of My Father who sent Me. My Father's will is simple. It is that I should not lose any of the people that He has given to Me. And this is the will of Him who sent Me, that everyone who sees the Son and believes in Him may have everlasting life; and I will raise him up at the last day" (John 6:27-40).*

After Andrea finished reading that latest news journal out loud, Claire asked her, "What's the beautiful one mean?" Andrea went into great detail about her incident in the creek and her vision of the garden. Explaining that in the vision, she would get further explanation on the Tree of Life, which is the Beautiful One. Then Andrea said, "Jesus Christ is the Beautiful One, He's the one that we are to look upon, and it is through His Holy Spirit that we do this. God has brought all of us here because He is drawing His people to Himself." Then once again, *The Way News Journal* disappeared right before Andrea's eyes.

As the two women walked on, all Andrea could think about was how and when her husband would come to know Jesus. Then those words from the vision that Jesus said to her flashed before Andrea's mind: "Marcus is a very good man."

**Discussion Questions:**

1) Those of the way: What was the significance of that phrase during the early church from the book of Acts?

Answer: The term "the Way," or "those of the way," was an early description of a sect of the Jewish faith who professed that Jesus died on the cross and rose from the dead three days later. One of their prominent identifiers was that they were filled with the Holy Spirit.

Additional scriptures on the Way: Acts 9:1-2, Acts 18:25-26, Acts 19:9 & 23, Acts 22:4, Acts 24:14. Then follow up with Acts 11:26.

2) In this chapter, Cliff asked Jeff, "Haven't you felt a peace while working around Jacob?"

   Some people say that there is a peace that passes all understanding when they turn their lives over to Jesus Christ. Where in the Bible can you find this described?

   Answer: Philippians 4:4-7; see also John 14:27 & 16:33.

3) In this chapter, Andrea said, "God has brought all of us here because He is drawing His people to Himself." Can you find a place in the Bible that emphasizes that God is calling His people out of the world?

   Answer: Acts 26:18 To turn them from darkness to light. See also John 1:1-5.

Scriptures: Acts 9:1-2, Hebrews 4:16, Romans 6:6-10, Luke 24:44-49, Mark 1:15, Psalms 51:1-4, II Corinthians 7:8-12, II Timothy 2:25-26, , John 6:27-40.

Discussion Question Scriptures: Acts 9:1-2, Acts 18:25-26, Acts 19:9 & 23, Acts 22:4, Acts 24:14, Acts 11:26, Philippians 4:4-7, John 14:27 & 16:33, Acts 26:18, John 1:1-5

# Chapter 16 ~ Friday

# Blessed are the Poor in Spirit

After lunch, Lucas walked into the mine and saw that Noah, the youngest of the four men loading the debris, struggled with his assignment. He had been unable to get his shovel load into the work cart, twice hitting the side and spilling the rocks on the ground. Then Lucas saw that all of the men were worn out from removing the debris, and he said to them, "You guys take the rest of the day off." Noah, Jacob, Cliff, and Jeff headed to the ranger station for a well-deserved reprieve. "Lucas is right. I don't think I could have shoveled another load of debris today," Noah said. "You got that right," Jacob said as the four men slowly made their way to the ranger station.

Back at the mine, Marcus and Lucas began the final debris removal along with the other rangers. Marcus said, "Thank you, Lucas, those guys were spent. I don't think they could've picked up another rock today." Lucas said, "We'll have this debris cleared out in no time; there's nothing like a fresh crew." As Keith was hauling out another load of debris, Jim, Steve, and Katie-Bird came over to assist Lucas and the other rangers since the shoring operation was completed.

Ding—Ding—Ding sounded the brass bell as Keith backed the train into the mine with the empty work carts. By that time, both Jim and Steve had become curious about the legitimacy of repeating the sinners' prayer. Steve asked Lucas, "If I repeated a sinners prayer once, how could those words have saved me?" Lucas asked him, "Steve, do you remember any of the words that you said in your sinners' prayer?" Emptying his shovel of debris into the work cart, Steve said, "I remember saying, 'I have been set free from sin and something about being a slave of righteousness,' but I never understood what that actually meant." Then Lucas asked, "How about you, Jim? Can you remember anything that you said when you prayed your sinners prayer?" "All that I remember is something about the wages of sin," Jim said while he scooped up another shovel load of debris. Then Lucas answered their question by saying:

"First of all, we should not sin just because we have the favor of grace. We bring ourselves into subjection to the one we serve, whether of sin leading to death or obedience leading to righteousness. We thank God though we were once bound by sin, now having obeyed from the heart a teaching that could deliver us. Steve, you have to search your own heart and decide if you have been set free from sin. It is the freedom from sin that enables you to become a servant of righteousness. Our flesh is weak, and sin is easy to fall into, leading to more and greater sin. Now that you have asked Jesus for His grace, you must pursue righteousness and holiness. When you lived according to the law of sin, you were free from the law of righteousness and holiness. But what did you gain by living in sin, knowing that the end result of sin is death? But now you have been set free from sin, and have become a servant of God. Now you do those things that lead to holiness, resulting in eternal life. But know and understand this, Jim, that the wages of sin are death, but the gift of God is eternal life in Christ Jesus our Lord. ([10] Romans 6:15-23).

**So, the question IS NOT: Was I saved when I said the sinners' prayer? But instead, is my heart longing for the grace of God today?"**

Keith hauled out that final load as the last of the debris was loaded into the work carts. Lucas noticed that this crew was also too tired to assist with the project that day, so he sent Jim, Steve, and Katie-Bird back to the ranger station, giving them the rest of the day off. Marcus couldn't help but listen to Lucas's words about the sinners' prayer. Marcus thought, "Wouldn't it be nice to be free from this burden that I carry. It's just too bad that my sin is so great." All that separated the crew from reaching the time capsule was two loads of rocks. However, those rocks were the ones that everyone had been dreading. They were what Lucas called—the big bad band of boulders.

Claire and Andrea continued to walk until they happened by one of the large rock piles. The trees provided a shady spot for the two women to stop and talk. Andrea said, "Jeff really responded to your prayer, and I think that is so amazing." Claire said: "Like I said at the pavilion the other day, 'I'll take the faith route.' I had a choice to make, and in desperation, I made it. Stay with my husband, put all my faith in God, or leave him and put all my faith in myself. It was your strength that encouraged me to pursue a life of faith in Jesus Christ. When you asked me if I wanted to pray for him, it was at that moment I knew prayer was the only hope that he had left in this world." As Claire spoke those words, tears began to stream down her face. She had become broken and contrite, hoping that her sorrow would soon be turned to joy.

As the two women sat there on the rock pile in the shade, Claire noticed a black box underneath some smaller rocks; she moved them aside, picking up the box. "Wow, that's simply beautiful. Don't you think so, Andrea?" The black box had golden lettering engraved on the top that said, "A MOTHERS LOVE," with a golden engraving of a mother holding two young children close to her heart. Andrea said, "Open it." Claire tried to open it. Then she said, "I can't; it seems to be locked." Claire handed the box to Andrea and said, "Here, you try." Andrea shook it, checking to see if anything was moving inside. "Oh my," Andrea said, and the box opened when she shook it. "What's in there?" Claire asked. "It's another edition of *The Way News Journal*," Andrea said. Then she began to read.

*My dearest Andrea, I am always with you and your children. The prayer that you spoke over your children has moved Me deeply. Your words transcended to my kingdom. Shortly I will bring about an event that will shake your husband, and it will also shake you. Andrea, you are going to question your faith, and you are even going to question Me. You will say to me, 'Lord, that wasn't fair.' Come, Andrea, listen to a story that I must tell you; Oh, you of little faith.*

> *There was a time when I got into a boat, and My disciples followed Me. We rowed for a long time. Then a great storm arose on the sea, and the boat was covered with the waves. But I was asleep, and my disciples believed that they would soon die. My disciples being fearful, came and woke me. I said to them, 'why are you so fearful, oh you of little faith.' Then I rose and rebuked the winds and the sea, and a great calm came upon the waters. My disciples marveled, asking who can do this, even the winds and the sea obey Him? (Matthew 8:23-27).*

***Andrea, you are my disciple, and you think that I have fallen asleep during your time of storm. Understand this; I am awake!***
***Your Lord and Savior***
***Jesus Christ***

And *The Way News Journal* disappeared before Andrea's eyes; however, the beautiful black box remained. Claire asked, "What do you think that means?" Andrea said, "I don't know." But she knew exactly what it meant.

Back at the ranger station, Jeff decided to take a nap before dinner. However, before he did, Claire made it back to the ranger station. Claire saw that Jeff was tired, and she said to him, "You look like you should get some rest." Jeff said, "There's nothing like a day of rock moving to make a man exhausted." By the time his head hit the pillow, Jeff was asleep and began to dream; this is the dream he had:

He was falling, and as he fell, he began to fall faster and faster until he could feel the wind flowing through his body. Then without any warning, he found himself falling through a tunnel. As Jeff fell, it became darker and darker. The darkness began to penetrate his body. Finally, he felt the deep darkness in his soul. He had this strange realization that the darkness was so powerful that he would never be free from it and could no longer tell if it was hot or cold. What seemed like hours of falling was finally complete. He had landed on the hard rocky ground. He tried to stand up, but he had a strange realization that every bone in his body had shattered when he hit the ground. As he lay there for what seemed like hours, he finally felt like he would be able to stand. And stand he did, but as he stood, he heard a voice calling his name. "Jeff Davis, I am the Son of man. You have rejected my calling upon your life. You have refused to allow the Holy Spirit to dwell in your temple. You have cast a judgment upon yourself (John 12:46-48). I called to you and said, 'come follow Me, you who labor and are heavy laden,' but you rejected My call (Matthew 11:28). You held your bitterness and your drunkenness to be a higher calling than the call of the Son of God. You will now spend eternity in the lake of fire as you have blasphemed my glorious Name. I am Jesus Christ, the Savior of all mankind." And at that moment, Jeff was cast alive into the lake that burns with fire and brimstone forever and ever (Revelation 19:20). At that moment, he could not distinguish between which was worse, the eternal torment of the fire and brimstone, or the complete eternal separation from Jesus Christ. Jeff knew he would be eternally tormented in a flame that would never die, and he was completely alienated from the love of God (Luke 9:42-48).

Claire was sitting in the next room at the table, eating her dinner when she heard Jeff's horrible screams coming from their room. Running into the bedroom, Clair said, "Jeff! Jeff, wake up, you're having a nightmare, wake up!" As Jeff awoke, he saw Claire's eyes looking into his. Jeff began to weep and cry as the dream was extremely real to him. Jeff explained the dream to Claire in great detail ending with the horror of being eternally separated from God. So, Jeff began to cry out to God like Claire had at the pavilion on Wednesday. Then Claire said to Jeff while she was cradling his head, "Blessed are the poor in spirit, For theirs is the kingdom of heaven" (Matthew 5:3).

**Discussion Questions:**

1) Have you ever said the sinner's prayer? In and of itself, that is not a problem. However, there was a discussion in this chapter about the legitimacy of saying the sinners' prayer. So, the question IS NOT: Was I saved when I said the sinners' prayer, but instead, is my heart longing for the grace of God today? How would you answer that question?

2) In this chapter, Jeff had a dream, and in the end, he found himself cast alive into the lake of fire. When you stand before Jesus Christ at the judgment, what will He say to you? See Matthew 11:28 & Revelation 19:20 for assistance.
   Answer: When I pass from this life, Jesus will say to me...

3) In this chapter, Jesus sent a news journal article to Andrea in response to a prayer she said to Him about her future children: "The prayer you spoke over your children has moved Me deeply." Have you ever said a prayer that you know has moved the heart of God?

Scriptures: Romans 6:15-23, Matthew 8:23-27, John 12:46-48, Matthew 11:28, Revelation 19:20, Luke 9:42-48, Matthew 5:3.
Discussion Question Scriptures: Matthew 11:28, Revelation 19:20.

# Chapter 17 ~ Friday

# Mentorship

Jacob, Noah, Jim, and Steve took advantage of the afternoon off. The four men were sitting outside the ranger station amongst the trees in the shade while a subtle breeze was blowing. Having been asked so many questions by Jim and Steve, Jacob thought this was the perfect opportunity to discuss mentorship with the other two men. Jacob said to them: "The Apostle Paul encouraged Timothy to be strong in the grace that is in Christ Jesus, referring to him as his son. Then Paul reminded Timothy to remember what he had taught him so that he would teach others like Paul had taught him" (II Timothy 2:1-2). Jacob continued by saying: "What I mean is this, take Noah for example, when he came to Christ, he needed a mentor, that is when I stepped in, just like Paul and Timothy. I knew that I must teach him the basics of the principles of God so he would become grounded in the faith. After a while, I was able to pull back as spiritual maturity set in. That is what I want for you two fellas. I want to mentor both of you in the faith until you grow into your own spiritual maturity. The last thing I want to see is one or both of you falling away from Jesus (Hebrews 6:1-8). The grace of God is fresh on you two, so what do you guys say?" Both Jim and Steve jumped at the chance to have a retired pastor become their mentor in the faith. Jim said,

"Jacob, I think this is a step in the right direction. I remember when I was a kid, no one followed up and offered to teach me anything further on growing in the knowledge of God." Steve had almost the same response. Noah said, "Cuz, it looks like you now have a church of three." Then all four men had a good laugh.

Word spread fast about Jeff's conversion at the mine. Lucas said to Keith, "I sure didn't see Jeff turning his life over to Jesus Christ." Before Keith had a chance to respond to Lucas, Marcus shifted everyone's attention back to the mine. He quickly changed the subject by walking over to several large boulders. Marcus said to Lucas, "What do you think we should do about your big bad band of boulders?" Lucas instinctively said, "That's easy, Boss; we'll just get some dynamite and blow them up." Marcus said, "I was thinking the same thing; does anybody have a plan B?"

By that time, Jacob and Noah had shown up back at the mine, checking on the progress. Marcus and Lucas looked at Jacob, thinking the older gentleman would have a plan to remove the boulders. While everyone looked at Jacob, he said, "Roll away the stone." He was referring to John 11:39 at the raising of Lazarus from the dead in a stone sealed tomb. Lucas said, "I already tried that one." "I know what I would do?" Noah said. A few moments passed, and no one said anything. Then Noah said again, "No, really, I have a plan." Noah, looking serious, got the attention of Marcus and Lucas as they both looked at him with anticipation of what the young man might have to say. Noah said: "I would start with the three small boulders using prybars to roll them onto the work carts while their sides are tilted over in the dump position. This will allow the weight of the boulder to set the work cart back into its locked upright position." "Okay, we've got a plan," Marcus said. With that, the crew went to work with Noah's plan to remove the boulders, starting with the three smaller ones. Keith backed the locomotive into the mine as close to the boulders as possible. He pulled the dump lever allowing the first work cart to tip to the side. Then the crew began the process of loading the smaller boulders into the work carts. Soon Keith hauled out the first load of boulders.

While Keith was away, Lucas and Jacob began a discussion. "I heard that Jeff accepted Jesus as his personal savior today," Lucas said. Jacob responded: "Yes sir, Jeff is now united to Him who was raised from the dead, bearing fruit to God. It was by the law that the knowledge of sin was made known to him. But now, by the newness of the Spirit, he has been released from following the letter of the law. Jeff died to sin and is living according to the Spirit." ([11] Romans 7:4-6). Noah looked at Jacob with a puzzled look on his face that said, "What did you just say?" Seeing the question in his eyes, Lucas said, "It's like this, Noah, we were set free from the need to follow the Law of Moses when the Holy Spirit was sent to dwell in our hearts. And it's the Holy Spirit rather than the Law of Moses that guides us to do the will of God." (Psalms 40:8, Romans 10:1-13, Galatians 2:16, Matthew 19:16-30). "Okay, that sounds better," Noah said, then he added, "I'll take the Spirit over the law any day." Jacob said to Lucas, "I couldn't have said it any better myself." The three men laughed as Keith backed the train into the mine once again with the brass bell sounding a warning to everyone, Ding—Ding—Ding.

Having realized that she had left her yellow hiking hat at the ranger station, Andrea returned to retrieve it. In doing so, she ran into Claire, who told her all about Jeff having accepted Jesus Christ as his Savior. Andrea said, "That's just wonderful, Claire. I'm so happy for both of you." Claire was so excited that she turned around and went back to see her husband saying nothing more to Andrea.

Having her yellow hiking hat with her, Andrea was making the twenty-minute walk back to the cabin. She stopped off at the pavilion along the way and began to pray, saying, "Lord, that wasn't fair. It was my husband who was supposed to get saved, not Claire's!" Then she heard a still small voice somewhere in her spirit that said to her, "Oh, you of little faith." Then Andrea began to weep as she remembered what God said to her in the news journal had just come to pass. She realized that Claire's sorrow had been turned into Joy. And for the first time, since God called Andrea back to Him, jealousy was ruling and guiding her heart rather than love. Andrea was tempted to question her own faith and God's ability to draw her husband to Him. She felt the presence of an evil spirit enticing her to stray from her faith and the truth of God. Then as she remembered the words of *The Way News Journal,* Andrea shouted, "It has been written, I will not live by bread alone, but I will live by every word that proceeds from the throne of God. I will worship the LORD my God, and Him only, I will serve" (Luke 4:8). Then Andrea remembered the words Claire said when she prayed for her husband and looked up to heaven and began to pray that same prayer by saying:

"Oh Lord, my heart cries out to You, Lord. Why is Your salvation so far away? I lift my husband up before You Lord—examine him—cleanse him—purge him—draw him near to You—fill him with Your Spirit—fill him with Your Holy Spirit Lord. I weep for Your grace. I weep for Your mercy. I weep for Your peace. How long must I wait? How long before Your salvation finds him? How long before his spirit is joined to Yours? Have mercy on him! Save him! Please, save him! Oh Lord, please save his soul!"

Back at the mine: All that separated the time capsule was the last three big bad band of boulders. "I think we will reach that time capsule soon," Marcus said. These next three boulders were bigger and more cumbersome than the others as the crew meticulously followed Noah's plan. After much effort, the last three boulders were loaded into the work carts. Keith stoked the fire in the boiler bringing the locomotive back to its maximum operating temperature. He was going to need full power to pull out this heavier load. Opening the main valve, Keith transferred power to the drive wheels, and the train began to move. "I was worried about that load," Lucas said. It was the heaviest yet. As the locomotive started hauling out the last of the big bad band of boulders, everyone began to cheer. Then they would haul out the time capsule, meeting their goal. POP—SCREECH—BANG!!! Suddenly, the mine train came to an abrupt stop. Then Keith yelled, "What the heck was that?!" Then everyone realized what had just happened. A wheel on one of the work carts had seized under the weight of the larger boulders pulling the two-track sections apart, destroying that portion of the track. Marcus knew there were no additional track pieces. He realized that making any repairs would be impossible before the annual Edwardsville community dinner on Saturday night.

Lucas stooped down and examined the damaged track sections. He could plainly see that it was caused by the rear wheel on the last work cart that had seized up under the additional weight of the larger boulders and had destroyed the track sections. Noah's heart sunk as he felt responsible for that mishap. Lucas asked, "Who was working on this work cart wheel? Noah stepped forward as if to face his accuser, and as he did, he heard a man's voice behind him say, "I am responsible. I never finished the wheel that I was working on. I just left it on the workbench. It's my fault. I take full blame," Marcus Peterson said. Marcus continued by saying, "We may have to postpone the dinner tomorrow night." Soon after, everyone left the mine feeling dejected as a sense of failure had overtaken their joy.

Later that evening at the cabin, Andrea had prepared dinner for Steve, Jim, and Katie-Bird Lewis. "That was a great meal, Mrs. Peterson," Katie-Bird said." Then she asked, "Andrea, where did you get that roast. Andrea shared with them that Marcus' boss had provided all the food for their trip. Then Andrea said, "Bird, you can just call me Andrea." And then she asked, "Why do they call you Bird when Katie is such a pretty name?" Katie-Bird said, "You don't know, do you?" "Know what?" Andrea asked as everyone else at the table broke out in a burst of laughter. "These two guys are my brothers. When I was a baby, my mother would sing to me, His Eye is on the Sparrow." Then she began to sing the song bringing tears to everyone's eyes, including Marcus. "By the time I was three, my mother would walk around the house singing, 'Where's my little Bird? Oh, where's my little Bird,' and it's stuck," she said. "I had no idea that you three were siblings," Andrea said. Then she asked, "Okay, that explains 'Bird,' but how did you guys get into construction?" Katie-Bird looked at her brother Jim and said with her eyes, "You take that one."

Jim spoke up and said, "Our mother and father were missionaries overseas. There was an earthquake in our village, and our building collapsed, trapping us inside. A rescue crew used heavy timbers to shore up the building to prevent additional collapses so they could rescue us. Steve and I were fascinated, and we became contractors when we grew up," Then Katie-Bird said, "I prayed that we would be rescued. You two boys relied on the natural, putting your faith in the wood and shoring. It was God who delivered us, not the shoring operation." Steve added to the conversation by saying, "What they didn't tell you was that we became orphans after the building collapse. Katie-Bird kept her faith, but Jim and I weren't as fortunate. We were older than her becoming hard and wanting to blame God for our loss. But it was Jacob and Lucas who brought us back to our faith." They all talked late into the night and were thankful for a night of fellowship. But Jim and Steve were thankful that they had found Jacob, a great man of God, to mentor them in the faith.

Later, the three siblings walked past the mine on their way back to the ranger station that night. And when they did, they noticed that the lights were still on inside. Katie-Bird said, "We should see what's going on in there." So, the three of them made their way into the mine, inquiring as to why the lights had been left on.

Later that night, at the cabin, Andrea was outside, sitting alone on the front porch while Marcus was inside. He was thinking about the incident at the mine that day. He made himself another plate of desert and sat down at the table. Then he thought, "What's this?" He had come across another edition of *The Way News Journal* lying in Andrea's open Bible, and he began to read.

**Discussion Questions:**
1) On mentorship: where are you in your life? Are you qualified to mentor, or do you still need a mentor to help you develop your faith? See II Timothy 2:1-2 for guidance. Notice that Timothy had already been taught by Paul and was ready to mentor others in the faith of Christ Jesus.
2) In this chapter, Jacob said, "It was by the law that the knowledge of sin was made known." However, Noah was puzzled by this explanation, and Lucas clarified the matter. He said, "It is the Holy Spirit rather than the Law of Moses that guides us to do the will of God." Can you remember when you

104

were confused about something in the Bible, and someone explained it in simple terms?

3) In this chapter, Andrea remembered Claire's prayer over her husband, praying the same over Marcus. Would you like to pray this same prayer over your spouse?

Scriptures: II Timothy 2:1-2, Hebrews 6:1-8, John 11:39, Romans 7:4-6, Psalms 40:8, Romans 10:1-13, Galatians 2:16, Matthew 19:16-30, Luke 4:8.

Discussion Question Scriptures: II Timothy 2:1-2.

# Chapter 18 ~ Saturday

# Sorrow Turned to Joy

J ust before the sun was expected to rise over the Cabin in the Way, Marcus was lying awake in bed. He thought: "Everything was fine yesterday afternoon. Now look at this project; there is no telling how long it will take to have enough material shipped from overseas to make the needed repairs to the track. I will have to call Mr. Bradford first thing this morning and update him on this latest development." As Marcus was still lying in bed, he was in the beginning stages of falling into self-pity. Then his alarm went off, reminding him that he wasn't going back to sleep any time soon. "Are you alright, honey?" Andrea asked. Then she rolled over in bed, falling back to sleep.

Soon, Marcus was sitting at the kitchen table, and he was once again looking over *The Way News Journal* that he found the night before. While pouring himself a cup of coffee, he thought, "What could this possibly mean,

*'Andrea, our heavenly Father, is drawing your husband to the Son of God.'*

"I should look this one up," Marcus said while he turned Andrea's Bible to Matthew 3:3 and read, "Prepare the way of the LORD; Make His paths straight." Marcus thought, "I just don't understand where Andrea is getting all of these news journals from." Then he heard the sound of the John Deere speeding by the front of the cabin. (John 1:6-13, Matthew 3:1-3).

Marcus went outside to meet Lucas, who was sitting in the John Deere. He said, "Are you ready, Boss? We've got a lot of work to do today." Lucas was a little more cheerful than Marcus had expected, considering the misfortune of the day before. "I'm coming," Marcus said reluctantly while he got in the John Deere. Then he asked, "Lucas, you're not going to spill my coffee this morning?" Then he thought, "Or are you?" Lucas pushed the gas pedal to the floor and said, "Hang on tight; I'm in a hurry." The two men tore off toward the red covered bridge at what seemed like 95 miles an hour with coffee flying everywhere. Marcus asked Lucas, "What's your hurry? We're not going to get this project done today!" Ignoring him, Lucas continued speeding to the mine. As Lucas sped across the red covered bridge, the last of Marcus's coffee launched out of his cup. Then Marcus thought, "Did the wheels just come off the ground?"

Soon after landing, Lucas parked the John Deere in front of the mine entrance, where the entire crew was waiting for their arrival. Noah was the first one to walk up to the John Deere and greet Marcus. "We got it done," Noah said, with a smile as wide as the Mississippi River. "You got what done?" Marcus asked. When Marcus saw the rest of the crew, he could see that they also had a smile on all of their face's a mile wide. Marcus asked him again, "You got what done, Noah?" "We got it done. You know, IT! We finished it," Noah said. But this time, he grabbed Marcus by the arm, pulling him out of the John Deere and leading him into the mine to show him what he meant while everyone else followed.

As Marcus walked into the still darkened mine, all that he could hear in the silence was the small rocks and pebbles crackling under his boots at every step. "CLICK," went Noah's little flashlight. The beam of light barely illuminated the ground at his feet. Then Noah let go of Marcus's arm, leaving him in almost total darkness. Marcus thought the silence was eerie. They continued to walk further into the mine, having only enough light to proceed. In a yelling whisper, Marcus asked, "Noah, what's going on in here?" Leading Marcus with his dimly lit flashlight,

Noah whispered back, "Shhh! You have to wait for it, Boss." Then Noah pointed his flashlight ahead to illuminate the area directly in front of them. There the silhouette of a figure appeared and was standing twenty feet ahead. At that moment, the mine's overhead lights came on, starting at the entrance, coming on one after the other until the entire work area was illuminated. There, in front of everyone and standing on the track, was Andrea. Marcus forgot, for the moment, why he was even there in the first place. He thought, "Wow, she is simply lovely." All Marcus could see was the overhead lights hitting her perfectly, shimmering off her beautiful hair. "Andrea, how did you get here?" Marcus asked. Andrea said, "Honey, you're missing the point." Marcus asked her, "What point?" He looked around and suddenly realized that the track had been repaired, the three large boulders had been removed, and the time capsule was loaded into one of the work carts. It was ready to be hauled out of the mine and displayed at the ranger station, right on schedule. In a moment of almost overwhelming gratitude, tears began to well up in Marcus's eyes as he did his best to conceal his emotions. As he looked around, he could barely take it all in. That moment had been his vision from the very start of that project.

Then Marcus asked, "But how? This project was a failure. I failed every one of you," Andrea, now standing at his side, held his arm in a moment of reassurance. Jacob stepped forward and said, to Marcus, "Late last night, we all got word that Noah was over at the mine working to straighten out 'the train wreck,' that's what we called it at dinner last night." Pointing to Noah, Jacob said: "This young man came up with a plan all on his own to put everything back in order. He got with Ranger Bruce, and they located enough rail track in one of the other abandoned mines to make the needed repairs. By that time, the whole team had assembled, and we fabricated the track in place and made all the repairs. And as you have already seen, the time capsule is loaded and ready to go."

Still confused, Marcus had one last question. He asked Andrea, "Yeah, but how…" Marcus could not finish his question because Lucas interrupted and said, "They don't call me slowpoke around here for nothing." Marcus was even more puzzled as he looked into Andrea's eyes to ask what that meant. Andrea said, "Just after you left the cabin with Lucas this morning, Ranger Bruce picked me up and gave me an E-ticket ride, taking a shortcut to the mine." "But Andrea, how did you know about all of this?" Marcus asked. Andrea answered, "Let's just say a little Bird told me late last night while I was sitting on the front porch." And at that, joy filled the atmosphere where gloom had ruled the day before.

Marcus looked at Jacob and said, "I'm sure you have come up with some kind of lesson from all of this."

Jacob said: "Well, as a matter of fact, there was a principal established in the repair of this track failure. And that is the law of Moses—the Ten Commandments—is useful to make known the sin in our hearts. The mere fact that we failed to meet our goal yesterday afternoon was an offense to all of us, just as sin is an offense to God. We could not have comprehended our despair until we experienced it, seeing the track section mangled. That track being destroyed represents the sin in our lives. The desire to repair the broken track section signifies repentance, which is a desire to change something in our lives that is out of order. During this project's darkest moment, we pulled together with the greatest desire to overcome after being made aware of our failure. Therefore, it was the law—the law of Moses—that represented the knowledge that the track had failed. That failure is to be compared to sin. This established the need to overcome—by repentance—that is, making right the wrong. We accomplished this in the natural by repairing the broken rail track sections. And we do this in the spirit through repentance by our faith in Jesus Christ." ([12] Romans 7:7-12). Then Jacob ended with, as he gestured to the now straightened train track, saying: "Prepare the way of the LORD; Make His paths straight" (Matthew 3:3). However, all that Marcus heard was, "Make His paths straight." Marcus thought, "That's more than a coincidence," knowing Jacob could not have had any knowledge of *The Way News Journal* that he had read that morning at the cabin.

Afterward, Andrea, Claire, and Katie-Bird, all agreed that the guys had the situation at the mine under control. They had decided to head down to the ranger station for some conversation over coffee and tea. However, on the hike to the ranger station, there was a quiet tension in the air as another one of those men wearing a hooded cloak was close behind them. Emanating from his being was the essence of holiness. The girls walked along in a deafening silence until they reached their destination.

All three women entered the ranger station and walked by Ranger Bruce, but Katie-Bird stopped and asked him, "Have you got my coffee ready yet, mister?" Ranger Bruce was beginning to have a crush on Katie-Bird, and she knew it. "I'll bring it right over to you," Ranger Bruce said. Then he said, "Oh wait, Andrea, you have another letter that just arrived." She walked back and took the letter from him. Then Andrea and Claire began making their drinks. Katie-Bird made her way to the table and waited for her coffee to be served. Soon Andrea and Claire joined Katie-Bird at the table. Ranger Bruce walked over to them, and after he handed Katie-Bird her coffee, he said, "I didn't see these when you ladies first walked in, but here they are." He laid two additional letters on the table, one addressed to Katie-Bird and the other one to Claire. Katie-Bird looked puzzled. However, Claire was beginning to be an expert. She explained what was happening in great detail before they opened the next edition of *The Way News Journal*. Each woman opened and read their letter aloud to the other two, starting with faith, then hope and finally love (I Corinthians 13:13).

*Faith—Katie-Bird: My Dearest Katie, when you were a child, you persevered through hardships, not wavering in your faith. You have continued to pray, developing a relationship with Me. I will guide you into the next season of your life. Always be strong in your faith.*
*All My Love, Jesus*

*Hope—Claire: My Dearest Claire, so very recently, you were living a life of despair that was void of hope. A path has been set before you and your husband that is straight and narrow, never wavering from Me. With each step you take, the Holy Spirit will guide you so that you never lose your hope.*
*All My Love, Jesus*

*Love—Andrea: My Dearest Andrea, you cringe at the thought of divorce, and justly so. You have committed yourself, your husband, your marriage, and your children to your heavenly Father, and I have answered your prayer. Now, Andrea, you must abide in faith, continue in hope, and always remain steadfast in love.*
*All My Love, Jesus*

Back at the mine, the crew began the process of tidying up the construction area and packing the remaining equipment back into the trailer. Jim and Steve started sharing how Jacob offered to mentor them in the faith with the rest of the guys. A light came on in Jeff's head as he, too, felt the need to be mentored in the faith. Jeff began to share his vision of falling into the pit of hell with Jacob, having no hope of salvation. Jacob said, "You see, Jeff, this is the fear of the Lord, and it is the beginning of knowledge and wisdom." (Proverbs 1:7 & 9:10). Jeff said: "There was a part in my dream where I was reaching for an empty canteen as I could feel my thirst increasing, but it was like no thirst that I had ever felt before. In my thirst, I was in anguish and utter despair and hopelessness and had lost all hope of salvation."

Then Jacob said: "What you were experiencing was your awareness of your need for salvation. This is found in the book of John, the fourth chapter, where Jesus met the Samaritan woman at a well. Jesus said to her, 'Give Me a drink,' representing the desires of the natural man. Jesus said to her again, 'If you knew who I am, you would've asked for living water.' The woman thought that Jesus was referring to the water in the well. Then Jesus made it plain that the water from the well would not satisfy the spiritual man. Jesus said, 'But whoever drinks of the water that I shall give him will never thirst. But the water that I shall give him will become in him a fountain of water springing up into everlasting life.' So, then the woman at the well said to Jesus, 'Sir, give me this water, that I may not thirst, nor come here to draw.' Jeff, in asking Jesus Christ to be your personal savior, you became born again, receiving that same living water that springs up into everlasting life. This is the same as the Samaritan woman at the well did so many centuries ago" (John 4:1-26). Then Lucas said, "Now, while we are talking about water, I should mention the need to be baptized."

**Discussion Questions:**
1) Can you remember a time in your life when you were being drawn to the Son of God? If yes, explain and, if no, see the Bonus Question below.
2) In this chapter, the law of Moses represented the knowledge that the track was broken. What was the crew's desire to repair the track said to be a representation of?
   Answer: Repentance; see Mark 1:14-15. This was described as making the wrong right by repairing the broken track section. Thus, giving a visual representation of repentance by seeing the rail track section made new. This is accomplished in the spirit through repentance by our faith in Jesus Christ.
3) In this chapter, Katie-Bird, Claire, and Andrea all received a news journal from I Corinthians 13:13. Of faith, hope, and love, which of these three is the greatest?
   Answer: Love. See also Mark 12:29-31, Luke 10:27-37, Colossians 3:12-14, I John 4:7-11.
4) Bonus Question—Jeff's dream explained: Can you imagine how it would feel for all eternity to know that you rejected the living water that is offered by Jesus? This is provided to all who humbly come to Him by way of repentance and faith, believing that Jesus is the Son of God.

Scriptures: John 1:6-13, Matthew 3:1-3, Romans 7:7-12, I Corinthians 13:13, Proverbs 1:7 & 9:10, John 4:1-26.

Discussion Question Scriptures: Mark 1:14-15, I Corinthians 13:13, Mark 12:29-31, Luke 10:27-37, Colossians 3:12-14, I John 4:7-11.

# Chapter 19 ~ Saturday

# Hide and Seek

A discussion about faith began after the three women finished reading the latest edition of *The Way News Journal*. Andrea said, "Without faith, there is no hope of pleasing Jesus Christ." Then she added: "That is precisely why I have been praying for an increase in my faith. I have begun to recognize where I have fallen short in believing that Jesus can perform that which He said He will do" (Hebrews 11:6). Katie-Bird said, "Andrea, I agree fully. For years, I prayed that my two brothers would not lose the faith in God they had acquired before our parents' death. And I can attest to you that He was faithful. My prayers have been answered. My brothers have returned to the faith." She took the last sip of her coffee and then held up her cup, gesturing to Ranger Bruce that it was empty. Then Katie-Bird said to Andrea: "You know, I was reading in I Thessalonians today, and I came across a passage that said that God is faithful to complete the work that He has started. I know that you are praying for your husband. Just continue to pray for him, never wavering. You see, Andrea, that is what I did for my two brothers. I continued to pray for them having faith that God would come through in the end." (I Thessalonians 5:23-24, James 1:2-8). Andrea took in everything that Katie-Bird said to her about faith, tucking it away in her heart. Then Katie-Bird said, "Now if you two ladies will excuse me, I have to go complain that the ranger on duty has not re-filled my coffee." They both laughed as Katie-Bird walked over to Ranger Bruce and said, "It's empty." She tapped her coffee cup with her fingernail, trying to get his attention. Ranger Bruce said, "I'm going to start my break. Would you care to join me?" The two of them walked outside to take advantage of the fresh mountain air with two hot cups of fresh coffee.

After finishing their coffee and tea, Andrea looked into Claire's eyes, and with tears flowing, she said, "You know Claire…" However, Katie-Bird interrupted her, not knowing that their conversation had turned serious just moments before. She said. "GIRLS! I have the key to the fallen-down office building." Then she waved her hand and said, "Come on, girls! It fell down during a blizzard that hit Edwardsville years ago. There's even a basement to explore." While the three women were on their way to explore the unknown, "Claire whispered to Andrea, "We'll finish our discussion later."

Back at the mine: Keith fired up the steam boiler, and before long, he began hauling the time capsule out of the mine. Soon, the locomotive pulled it outside, stopping next to where Lucas had parked the John Deere earlier. It took four of the men to transfer the time capsule to the John Deere. "That side is a little tight," Noah said while they were loading it. "Is that better?" Jim asked after making an adjustment. "I think we got it," Keith said. "Okay, slow as you go, Lucas," Marcus said as he closed the tailgate. The crew was about to make the trip to the ranger station classroom with the time capsule finally loaded into the John Deere. Marcus thought, "This is sure a turn of events. I thought today was going to be a disaster of a day, but here we are making the victory march." Then he said, "Lucas, don't even think about going fast. In fact, I'll just walk in front of you, and you can follow me." Lucas smiled as he had planned to go at a snail's pace so the time capsule would not be damaged. While the crew and the John Deere were on their way to the ranger station, Noah said to Jacob, "I sure thought that time capsule was going to be bigger." Jacob said, "So did I. From my perspective, it's about the size of an oven."

Meanwhile, the women were making their way into the fallen down office building. As they did, they came upon the locked door that Ranger Bruce told them about. "Are you sure that's the right key?" Claire asked. "Yes, I'm sure. Ranger Bruce said to push it in all the way and pull the key back just a little bit. Then turn it to the left, all the while pulling the door tight against the jamb," Katie-Bird said. "You mean like that?" Andrea asked. "Oh, I think I got it," Katie-Bird said. Then she said, "Yes, I did it; we're in." Then the three women descended the rickety stairs, all the while staying close to the handrail. It got darker and darker as they slowly made their way down into the basement. Only a small amount of light emanated from a little window near the top of the basement wall. "Wow, this is amazing," Claire said. Andrea said, "It certainly is. You know, Claire, Lucas never mentioned to us about the basement." She was referring to when she and Claire had toured the fallen down office building the day before.

"It's like a museum down here," Katie-Bird said. As the three women walked along an open area, they came upon a stone archway that led to a small hallway with three doors, two of which were opened. However, one was closed with an opened padlock hanging on the latch. "Let's go in that room," Claire said, pointing to the door with the opened padlock. "But the sign says, 'KEEP OUT,'" warned Andrea, gesturing to the sign. "I know," Claire said. She removed the padlock tossing it to the ground. Then she opened the door anyway, going inside as the two other women reluctantly followed her. "This room is a lot darker than the other room," Claire said while walking ahead. The only light in that room was coming from the opened door. "I can't see anything," Claire said, who was now about twenty feet ahead of the other two women. She continued to go on, pressing farther into the darkened room. "I can't see Claire anymore. Can you see her, Andrea?" Katie-Bird asked. Then they heard a scream with a loud thud following immediately after. Andrea shouted, "What was that! Claire, are you okay? Claire, can you hear me!?" Katie-Bird asked, "Andrea, do you have a flashlight?" "No," she answered.

Katie-Bird once again shouted, "CLAIRE, WHERE ARE YOU!?"

Meanwhile, the crew had almost finished transporting the time capsule to the ranger station. BeeP—BeeP—BeeP went the backup alarm. "Sorry, Boss, this is what happens when I back up," said Lucas while he backed up to the ranger station's classroom door. With one finger in his ear to deafen the backup alarm and the other hand gesturing for Lucas to continue backing, Marcus said, "That's okay, Lucas, we've got all day."

"STOP," Marcus shouted. Lucas had backed up as far as he could. Soon after, four of the men were carrying the time capsule into the classroom. Cliff said, "This thing sure is heavy." Noah said, "It had to be to withstand that collapse." Keith said, "It may be the size of an oven, but it sure weighs a ton."

The curator for the annual Edwardsville community dinner, George Fields, said to Marcus, "I can't believe you and your crew managed to pull this project off without a single hitch." Marcus looked at Lucas, and they both looked at the rest of the crew. Everyone got a good chuckle out of his understatement. George sensed 'the without a single hitch' part wasn't totally accurate. Then George said, "Okay, the main thing is that you guys pulled it off. George realized the four men were still holding the time capsule, and he said to them, "Sorry guys, you can set it down on the floor." The four men sat the time capsule down in the middle of the classroom. George asked, "So, Marcus, where did you put the time capsule stand?" "Stand, what stand?" Marcus asked.

Meanwhile, the women continued to make their way through the darkened room. Katie-Bird shouted, "Andrea, I can't see anything. Claire, where are you? Can you hear us?" "I'm over here. I tripped over a box that was lying on the floor," Claire said. "Are you okay?" Andrea asked. "Yes, I think I'm fine now. I just got disorientated in the darkness after I fell," said Claire. Soon, Andrea and Katie-Bird were by her side, helping Claire to her feet. Andrea began feeling for a light switch along the wall, and Katie-Bird checked for a flashlight on the table in the windowless room. Katie-Bird said, "I found some candles and matches." She struck a match, lighting three candles, giving one to Claire and one to Andrea.

Claire picked the box up off the floor that she had tripped over. She said, "I don't want anyone else to trip over this box." Then the box fell out of her hand, spilling its contents onto the table. "What's that?" Katie-Bird asked. She picked up one of the items to examine it by the light of her candle. "I think it's a letter," Andrea said. Then Claire said, "No, it's a page torn out of a Bible. It looks like it's from I John chapter three." Andrea asked, "What else fell out of the box?" Holding her candle over the table, Katie-Bird said, "There are some hand-written letters." Andrea asked, "What do they say?" Bringing her candle closer to one of the letters, Katie-Bird began to read it aloud.

> My dearest Lord and Heavenly Father, hear my supplication as I come before Thee in prayer. My sin is always before Thine eyes, this wretched man that I am. I long to be pure in Thy sight, but I fear I have fallen short of Thy righteousness. If Thou would bid me this one petition: Thy grace Lord, Thy grace; I plead, extend to me Thy grace my Lord. This is my cry, this is my plea as my tears wash over me, that Thou would extend Thy grace to a wretch such as I. While I weep before Thee upon my knees, let nothing come between me and Thee except Thy grace. Then I will walk before Thee in holiness with a pure heart.
>
>> For innumerable evils have encompassed me about: mine iniquities have taken hold upon me so that I am not able to look up; they are more than the hairs of mine head: therefore, my heart faileth me. Psalms 40:12 [KJV]

"I wonder what he did that was so bad?" Claire asked. Katie-Bird said, "There's no telling." However, Andrea had a sense of the depth of that man's faith. She remembered the discussion she had with Katie-Bird earlier at the ranger station, but this time Andrea knew that her faith would have to come from a pure heart.

Back at the ranger station classroom, George said to Marcus, "Since you don't know anything about the time capsule stand, I'll take some of your guys to the storeroom, and we'll look for it there." So, Jacob, Noah, Jeff, and Cliff went with George to look for the time capsule stand.

George gave a little history lesson about the time capsule while the men walked to the storeroom. He said, "The time capsule was sealed up when the town of Edwardsville opened the School in the Way many years ago. So, as you may have already guessed, there is no longer anyone left around here who knows what's inside of it." Then stopping at the door, George said, "We have to go through here to get down to the storeroom, and all four men followed. "It's a little dark in here," Noah said, and he turned on his little flashlight. "Noah, it looks like your flashlight only made it darker in here," Cliff said, teasing him. Soon enough, and with Lucas's little flashlight guiding them, the men made it down the stairs into the storeroom. After turning on the light, George found the time capsule stand. Then he said, "Okay, it's a little on the heavy side, so be careful when you pick it up. As the four men maneuver to lift it, Jacob asked, "Do you guys have it?" Then at the same time, both Noah and Cliff yelled, "NO!" Then the time capsule stand slipped from their hands, crashing to the ground with a loud noise: Ka-BAM—BANG—THUD! Then Andrea asked Clair and Katie-Bird, "What was that noise?!" The women were surprised by the sudden crashing sound that shook the floor that they were standing on.

After the four men dropped the time capsule stand, George said, "Don't worry, guys, that thing's indestructible; that's why it's so heavy. Noah said, "I think we can get it this time. We just weren't ready for how heavy it was." While making a second attempt at lifting it, Noah said, "I think we got it now." The four men carried the time capsule stand while George led the way. "We'll go through here," said George. He opened a door leading the men into another darkened room. CLICK went George's flashlight as his beam of light penetrated the darkness leading them to the stairs on the other side of that room. "Set that stand down here!" George said as he halted in the center of the room. George asked the other men, "Do you guys smell something burning down here?" "Yes, I smell something. It smells like burning candle wax," Jeff said. Just then, and from underneath the table, Claire said, "Jeff, is that you?" George shined his flashlight on the three women who were hiding under the table. "Hey, what are you three ladies doing under there? And how did you get into the historical archives room?" George asked. Speechless, the women made their way out from underneath the table with the assistance of the guys. Claire explained by saying, "The padlock was opened, so we just thought we would explore." Claire felt responsible for having pressed the other two women to enter that room. With a stern look on his face, George said, while his face transitioned to a warm smile, "That's okay, ladies, we get people exploring down here all the time." Then George reached up and pulled a long string hanging directly over the table attached to a light illuminating the room.

"Did you ladies find anything of interest down here?" George asked. Looking up at the light directly over the table, the three women laughed simultaneously. Then Katie-Bird said, "We found this letter, but it doesn't make any sense." After reading the letter, George said, "This letter was written by Daniel Edwards." Andrea and Claire locked eyes as it clicked that they had read about Daniel at the ranger station the day before. Then George addressed the entire group explaining about Daniel and the letter that the women had just found and read:

He is the man responsible for building the cabin that Andrea and Marcus are staying in this week. Daniel first intended it to be a church, and it was going to be called the Church in the Way. However, Daniel died before it was completed. It sat dormant for many years until the townspeople decided that it must be finished and made into a school. When the building was completed, it was called the School in the Way. Years later, the townspeople decided to name the town after Daniel, calling it Edwardsville.

Most of the items in this archive room are from Daniel's journals. He was a humble man of God, always desiring to be closer to his Lord. Daniel didn't hold himself to the light of men. Instead, he held himself to the light of God. That is why the letter seemed to have a conflicting message. If we were to hold ourselves to the same standard that Daniel Edwards did back then, we too would fall down on our faces and cry out to God for his grace. I always turn to the Bible whenever I read one of Daniel's letters. In this letter, he seemed to be full of sin, and at the same time, walking in the light of God. The Apostle John said that we no longer sin once we are born of God (I John 3:4-9). This makes it sound like once we are saved, we never sin again. However, the Apostle Paul seemed to have a different argument. He said, "With the mind I myself serve the law of God, but with the flesh the law of sin." One thing is for sure, the Bible does not contradict itself. Essentially Daniel was saying that the Spirit that dwells within us never sins. When we are born again, we become the temple of the Holy Spirit. ([13] Romans 7:21-25, I Corinthians 6:19). As Paul said in Romans 7:22, "For I delight in the law of God according to the inward man." In Galatians 5:16. It says, when we walk in the Spirit, we don't walk in the deeds of sin. It is our flesh nature that works against the Spirit, thus making them contrary to one another. So basically, Daniel Edwards said, his old nature made him feel unworthy compared to God. But it was the Holy Spirit that made him feel there was purity in his life.

"Thank you," Claire said, "you really helped us." George said, "No, thank you. It was you ladies who helped us. You took the padlock off of the door, and now we don't have to go the long way back to the ranger station."

**Discussion Questions:**
1) Without faith, there is no hope of pleasing Jesus Christ—Hebrews 11:6. Sometimes in life, a person has to put their faith in Jesus Christ when they hope for a loved one's salvation. Is there a loved one you need to pray for in your life? Do you

believe Jesus has begun to work in their life? If so, do you also believe that He will finish it? (I Thessalonians 5:23-24).

2) In this chapter, the women found a written prayer of Daniel Edwards. "My sin is always before Thine eyes." Can you find any passages in the Bible where men felt God's presence when they stood before Him?

Answer: Isaiah 6:1-7, Daniel 10:1-9, Revelation 1:9-17. These same scriptures are found in discussion question (# 1) from chapter 2.

3) Two apostles make a statement that seems to contradict one another. (I John 3:9, & Romans 7:13-25). How can both of these men be right?

Answer: When we are born again, we don't sin as a lifestyle because the Holy Spirit within us never sins. This is according to the new birth. But when we do sin, we have an advocate with the Father—Christ the Lord. (I John 2:1, John 3:5, I John 1:9)

Scriptures: Hebrews 11:6, I Thessalonians 5:23-24, James 1:2-8, Psalms 40:12, I John 3:4-9, Romans 7:21-25, I Corinthians 6:19, Galatians 5:16.

Discussion Question Scriptures: Hebrews 11:6, I Thessalonians 5:23-24, Isaiah 6:1-7, Daniel 10:1-9, Revelation 1:9-17, I John 3:9, Romans 7:13-25, I John 2:1, John 3:5.

# Chapter 20 ~ Saturday

# The Portion of the Wicked

W hile the crew was retrieving the time capsule stand,
Marcus caught up on some paperwork at the ranger
station. Finding the rail track delivery invoice, Marcus
put it on the stack that he had designated as "need to file." Then a
soft wind filled his office as one of those hooded men walked past
Marcus' office on his way out of the ranger station classroom.
Then Marcus took a sip of his freshly poured coffee, and after
placing it back on the coaster, he chose the next document to
process. When he did, he discovered that it was another edition of
*The Way News Journal*. However, this time it was addressed to
him.

*Dear Marcus, I have been sent by God to explain your need for
salvation more clearly and the dangers of rejecting the saving
power of the blood of the Lamb. Marcus, no one who defiles or is
a liar, will have his name written in the book of life. Your name,
Marcus, is in danger of being blotted out of God's book. Be
warned those who stand before Jesus whose names are not found
written in the book of life will be cast into the lake of fire. If you
can overcome your secret sin that you still carry, the Lord of
heaven will put a white garment on you, and He will not blot your
name from the Book of Life written from the foundation of the*

*world. Remember, you will rejoice when you accept the Holy Spirit because your name is written in heaven. Seek the Lord and ask where the good way is and walk in it; then you will find rest for your soul. But fire and brimstone and a burning wind shall be the portion of the wicked. (Revelation 21:27, Exodus 32:31-33, Revelation 20:15, Psalms 90:8, Revelation 3:5, Luke 10:20, Jeremiah 6:16, Psalms 11:6).*
*Yours truly the servant of the Lord Jesus*
*Gabriel*
*P. S.*

*Marcus, if you are not born again, you will only feed your family from the corrupted nature of the tree of the knowledge of good and evil. You need to become humbled and broken, calling on the name of the Lord Jesus.*

Once Marcus finished reading the news journal, his coffee was cold. Then without any further thought, he placed the news journal in the pile of papers that he had designated as "need to file." However, Marcus couldn't help but remember those conversations with Andrea during this trip. There was the dream where he nailed Jesus to the cross. Andrea's encounter in the garden with Jesus as a result of her falling into the creek. Andrea's insight of Jason and Katie, their future children, through her dream and *The Way News Journal*. Then Marcus remembered those words Andrea said to him, "Marcus, what is it that you just can't let go of?"

Andrea and Claire were sitting at the pavilion while Katie-Bird assisted the guys with the time capsule stand. Claire said, "Andrea, we didn't finish our conversation from earlier." Andrea said, "Yes, your right." Then she paused while turning her head down and said: "I have to admit to you that I was offended when I found out that Jeff had accepted Jesus as his savior. You told me that I was a lucky woman the other day, and I felt blessed. Now you're the lucky one, and I'm the one still praying for my husband to come to know Jesus as his savior. I was even warned that I would feel this way. It happened just like God said it would in the news journal article. Then once I recognized what I was doing, I realized that I had never poured my heart out before God for my husband like you did. So, I prayed for Marcus like you prayed for Jeff. I hope you can forgive me for being jealous." Claire said, "To be honest with you, Andrea, it's okay that you felt that way. In all reality, that's how I felt about you when we first met. That's why I said, 'you're a lucky woman.' Now while we're alone, why don't you pray for Marcus." Then Andrea got down on her knees and prayed for her husband, saying:

"Dear Heavenly Father, I come before You in prayer, seeking a way for my husband to bring his heart, soul, and mind into alignment with You, Lord. Open his eyes so that he turns from the tree of the knowledge of good and evil. Enable him to feed our family spiritually from the tree of life, the beautiful one. I know Marcus is a good man, and I lift him up before You. Please, allow him to be released from this burden that he carries, whatever it may be." (Matthew 22:36-40, Acts 26:18).

Andrea and Claire sat at the pavilion for a while, savoring all they had said and thought. At that moment, a lifelong friendship had begun.

George was leading the way as the other men brought the time capsule stand to the ranger station. Lucas and Katie-Bird were assisting as well. "I agree," Jacob said. Responding to Lucas's statement on baptism. "You mean to tell me that baptism is like a marriage ceremony?" Cliff asked. SLAM went the John Deere's tailgate as the men had decided that the time capsule stand was too heavy to be carried by hand to the ranger station. "Slow as you go, Lucas," Jacob said. Soon enough, Katie-Bird yelled, "STOP!" Lucas had backed the John Deere as close to the classroom door as he could.

The four men carried the time capsule stand into the classroom. As they did, they walked by the opened door of Marcus's office, where he was still sitting at his desk. Jacob said to the others: "It was the Holy Spirit, the Spirit of the Father that raised Jesus from the dead. When we are baptized, we symbolize the death, burial, and resurrection of Jesus in a ceremony just like a man and a woman would do at their wedding. The act of baptism doesn't save anyone because the work of salvation can't require a component that relies upon an act performed by a person." Cliff asked, "Why should I be baptized if it's only a ceremony?" George said: "After the people were baptized by John, confessing their sins by repenting, Jesus himself was baptized by John, thus setting an example for all of us to follow. But remember, Cliff, many local churches provide classes on water baptism. It would be a good idea to attend one of those to receive the needed teaching." Then Jacob answered, "Just remember one thing, when you stand before Him on judgment day, you will be the one explaining to Jesus why you chose not to be baptized." (Matthew 3:13-17, Mark 1:1-11). Then Jacob said, "So your right, Lucas, the only role that a man played in salvation was the Man Christ Jesus from the cross." Lucas replied to the group by saying, "Once we take on the nature of Jesus by denying our sin nature, we are no longer under condemnation. The Spirit of Christ Jesus has made us free from the law of sin and death." ([14] Romans 8:1-11, Matthew 28:19-20, Acts 2:38).

After hearing the men's conversation about Jesus and baptism while carrying the time capsule stand into the classroom, Marcus walked out of his office. Then the men sat the time capsule on the stand. Marcus said to them all, "The time capsule sure looks great sitting on its stand." In making that statement, Marcus refused to acknowledge, to his own heart, that he had heard any part of their discussion about baptism or Jesus Christ.

**Discussion Questions:**

1) In this chapter, who can Marcus be represented by from the Bible?
   Answer: The prodigal son. All that he needs to do is return to his heavenly Father, and Jesus will receive him and give him a new name. (Luke 15:11-32, John 1:12, Ephesians 3:14-19, Revelation 3:12).

2) Can you think of another representation from scripture for Marcus from the news journal in this chapter?
   Answer: the parable of the lost sheep (Luke 15:1-7).

3) What do you think about water baptism? Have you ever been water baptized? And what is the proper sequence of baptism?

Answer: Repent, and let every one of you be baptized in the name of Jesus Christ for the remission of sins; and you shall receive the gift of the Holy Spirit (Acts 2:38).

4) By what authority was Jesus raised from the dead?
   Answer: It was the Holy Spirit. The Spirit of the Father had the authority to raise Jesus from the dead (Romans 8:11).

Scriptures: Revelation 21:27, Exodus 32:31-33, Revelation 20:15, Psalms 90:8, Revelation 3:5, Luke 10:20, Jeremiah 6:16, Psalms 11:6, Matthew 22:36-40, Acts 26:18, Matthew 3:13-17, Mark 1:1-11, Romans 8:1-11, Matthew 28:19-20, Acts 2:38.

Discussion Question Scriptures: Luke 15:11-32, John 1:12, Ephesians 3:14-19, Revelation 3:12, Luke 15:1-7, Acts 2:38, Romans 8:11.

.

# Chapter 21 ~ Saturday

# The Saving Knowledge of

After helping the guys move the time capsule stand, Katie-Bird left the ranger station and had hoped to catch up with Andrea and Clair. While walking along the second marked trail and holding her news journal article, Katie-Bird thought, "I'm just not sure about these letters." Then she stopped to read it one more time. She knew in her heart that it was an accurate depiction of her life. She thought, "I did persevere through hardships, I never wavered in my faith, and I developed a relationship with Jesus." Soon enough, Katie-Bird saw the other two women sitting at a picnic table. Then she put her news journal article back into her pocket.

Stopping at the pavilion, Katie-Bird said to Andrea and Clare, "I was hoping that you two would be here." She took the news journal out of her pocket and said, "I don't know what to think about these." Andrea said, "I can't explain where they come from, but I have come to appreciate them." Claire said, "I was apprehensive at first, especially when we found one in a bottle floating on the lake. I'm okay with them now." Katie-Bird said, "You know, I have come to feel a sort of peace about them." She laid her news journal on the picnic table and read it to the others. Then she said, "Even though I lost him when I was young, my father instilled faith as a value in my life. He taught me faith didn't always come quickly or easily. Sometimes in life, you have to persevere through hard times and really dig deep down and press through." Andrea added, "Yes, you mean like Abraham and Isaac?" Katie-Bird said, "That was a tough faith call, but Abraham pressed through gaining the favor of God (Genesis 22:1-19). When my brothers lost their faith, I had to hold on to mine, sometimes the line was thin, but I never let go." Andrea thought, "My faith is thin, alright." Then she asked Jesus, saying to herself, "Lord, is my faith a rope, a string, or is it just a thread that could snap at any moment?" But as Claire began to speak, Andrea knew she wasn't going to get an answer anytime soon.

Claire pulled her news journal article out of her pocket and read it to the other two women. Then she said, "I was all out of hope, but when I got here, my hope revived. When I was a child, my grandmother would read stories to me about children who were orphans." Claire paused for a moment as she turned her head down, then the tears began to stream from her eyes. Andrea asked, "Claire, were you an orphan?" Unable to speak, Claire nodded her head as Katie-Bird began to console her since she also knew what it was like to be an orphan. The tears turned into sobs while the moments flew by. The three women watched the wind blow through the tops of the trees while the birds sang out a few familiar melodies. Then regaining her composure, Claire said: "The other day, hope came rushing in like never before. In fact, I didn't remember what hope even felt like until a few days ago. I was void of all hope, but now my hope gets stronger every day. My grandmother was unable to care for me as she got older. As a result, I spent most of my time in the orphanage. After she passed, I would lay in bed, thinking about the stories of Jesus and the children. It was right here," Claire paused as she gestured with her arms to the pavilion. The tears began to flow, and she fell into a sob again for a few moments. Then she said, "It was right here where hope flooded back into my life when I said, 'I'll take the faith route.'" "I remember," said Andrea as she grabbed Claire's hand. Then wiping away the tears, Claire said, "Well, that's my story, and I'm sticking to it." Then a smile appeared on Claire's face as laughter penetrated her sorrows of yesteryear. Claire had let go of her past, and Andrea recognized it through the peaceful expression on her face. Andrea longed for the day that Marcus would do the same. Andrea teetered with unsure hope that Marcus would one day let go of his past sin that was hindering him from a life of God and peace. She questioned herself, "Am I going to fall into doubt, or will I choose to be full of hope?"

Claire and Katie-Bird directed their attention to Andrea. She knew that it was her turn to read her news journal article or to be silent. Then with a slight dip of her head, Andrea closed her eyes as she had chosen silence. Once again, the sound of the birds filled the air while a slight breeze blew the few remaining spring leaves across the pavilion floor. As the wind swept leaves rattled around aimlessly, the temperature suddenly began falling. Andrea lifted her head as she closed her jacket to ward off the falling temperature.

Then Andrea began to speak, saying: "When I was a young girl, my parents divorced. Before that day, I thought I knew what love was, but my notions were shattered in the divorce. I had lost my faith, my hope was gone, and my love had died. I remained in that state until I met Marcus. Everything was great until I had a dream of him nailing Jesus to the cross on the morning of our wedding. That's when I felt that something was amiss. Then I remembered the promise that I had made to God as a child. I said, 'Lord, I will love you all the days of my life if you would just bring happiness back into my parents' lives.' Well, God lived up to his part of my bargain. After their divorce, my parents were happy, very happy, even became good friends. However, my expectations were for them to be happy together in marriage living in the same home. God has shown me this past week that true happiness revolves around Him. Our future children will need a father who is a godly man. During this past week, I have placed my faith, hope, and love back into the hands of my heavenly Father. Now I know He has heard my prayers." Both Claire and Katie-Bird silently prayed that Andrea would not lose faith, hope, or love.

Katie-Bird said, "Andrea, your faith, hope, and love have been revived just like Jesus at the resurrection." Claire leaned in and listened more attentively. Then Katie-Bird said, "The disciples lost faith, were void of hope, and felt abandoned by love when Jesus died on the cross. But when He resurrected, hope was restored, love abounded, and they became steadfast in faith for the rest of their lives." Andrea said, "I never looked at it like that before, but you're right; something changed with them after the resurrection." Claire said, "It was the Holy Spirit." Andrea said, "Yes, it was the Holy Spirit." Katie-Bird said, "When the disciples received the Holy Spirit, faith, hope, and love were magnified by the indwelling Spirit of the Father. That's when they began doing the greater works that Jesus said they would do" (John 14:12-14). The three of them sat for a few moments as the thoughts of that discussion sank into their hearts. Soon after, Andrea looked at her watch and said, "It's getting late. I should be leaving to get ready for tonight's dinner at the ranger station."

After Marcus commented on the time capsule stand at the ranger station classroom, Jacob continued speaking to the construction crew and Marcus. Jacob said: "Once we take on the nature of Christ, we no longer live according to the flesh because we live according to the Spirit of God, becoming sons of God. Sometimes we even suffer with Christ. In the end, we will be glorified with Him." ([15] Romans 8:12-17). Marcus asked, "So, Jacob, you mean to tell me that we suffer, and that is of God?" Jacob said: "God doesn't promise a life of prosperity here on earth, but He did tell us that we will suffer with Him. In the book of Acts, God said of Paul, 'For I will show him how many things he must suffer for My name's sake.'" (Acts 9:16). Then Jacob said: "So, Marcus, because the Apostle Paul suffered for Christ, a good portion of the New Testament was written. Which has led to countless millions of people committing their lives to Jesus Christ. And it was in Paul's suffering that he pressed deeper into prayer, thus being led by the Holy Spirit in a greater measure of faith." Marcus thought on that last statement, unable to press it out of his mind for the moment. Then George said, "If you gentlemen will excuse me, I have to get with the caterers and see when they will arrive with the food." George left the other men as the rangers began setting the classroom up for dinner that night. Then the construction crew also left the ranger station. As they did, Marcus and Keith left together. While walking, Keith opened up to Marcus, telling him about his story of redemption.

As Andrea was walking alone to the cabin along the second marked trail, she heard a voice in her head, "ANDREA— ANDREA! MARCUS WILL NEVER COME TO THE SAVING KNOWLEDGE OF...

**Discussion Questions:**

Note: See chapter 18 for these *News Journal* articles.

1) FAITH: Katie-Bird said, "Faith doesn't always come quickly." In your lifetime, have you placed all of your faith in Jesus Christ?

2) HOPE: Claire said, "I didn't think I had any hope, but when I got here, my hope revived." Have you ever experienced a time in your life when your hope was revived?

3) LOVE: Andrea said, "I thought I knew what love was, but my ideas were shattered." Have you ever been in a situation similar to Andrea, where your ideas of love were shattered? If so, how did you overcome it?

4) Of the three; faith, hope, and love, which of these is the greatest?

Answer: The greatest is love (I Corinthians 13:13).

Scriptures: Genesis 22:1-19, John 14:12-14, Romans 8:12-17, Acts 9:16.

Discussion Question Scriptures: I Corinthians 13:13.

# Chapter 22 ~ Saturday

# We are More Than Conquerors

Lucas said, "George, they're here!" George replied, "Great, I'll go and let them in the back door, and they can get set up." George was referring to the catering company; they had just arrived, being right on time. George unlocked the back door of the ranger station, and they began the process of bringing in all the food for that night's event. Then Lucas said, "George, I'll see you in a few minutes. I'm going to the cabin to pick up Marcus and Andrea."

Meanwhile, Marcus and Andrea were ready and waiting for Lucas' arrival at the cabin. They discussed their plans that were to occur that next day when their honeymoon was to officially begin. Soon, Lucas arrived, interrupting their honeymoon planning session. After Lucas went inside, Andrea said to him, "YOU ARE GOING TO GO SLOW!" She was dressed in an evening gown for that night's event. Lucas said, "Yes ma'am, they don't call me 'slow as you go Lucas' around here these days for nothing." The three of them walked outside, and Marcus assisted Andrea into the John Deere's front seat, and he took the back. "You touch that gas pedal before I'm ready, and you have had it, Mister," Andrea said with a look that could kill, quickly turning into a smile and ultimately transitioning into a warm burst of laughter. Lucas, running on fear, looked at her with a smile and said, "Slow as you go, Lucas," as he gingerly pressed the accelerator. Then the three of them made their way to the ranger station.

The townspeople were arriving at the ranger station for the dinner and time capsule reading. They were looking forward to finally knowing what was inside the time capsule after all those years. Jeff and Claire, along with the rest of the crew, were in attendance as well. While everyone was mingling and having a great time, Lucas arrived with Marcus and Andrea. The three of them walked in together, greeting the people of Edwardsville. Soon enough, the attendees began to assemble at the various tables set up in the classroom. As Marcus stood in front of the time capsule, he took advantage of that transition moment before the evening officially began.

As the events of the past week flashed through his head, there was only one that stood out as the defining moment. It was when Noah took the lead in making the repairs to the track. With his hand on the time capsule, Marcus came out of his daze when he realized Noah was standing in front of him. Marcus said, "Noah, it's because of you that we are here tonight. In fact, if it weren't for you, I would be spending next week trying to convince my boss to keep me on the payroll." Noah had become a very humble man after all the things he had suffered through. Noah said, *"Yet in all these things, we are more than conquerors through Him who loved us."* ([16] Romans 8:37). Marcus was speechless that time, having no thought in his heart contrary to Noah's statement. He just looked at the young man and said in a humble tone, "Thank you, Noah, for all that you have done on this project." Then gaining everyone's attention, George said, "Ladies and gentlemen, may I have your attention, please? Dinner is now being served in the classroom."

Before long, everyone was seated, and the catering company served the meals. Marcus and Andrea were sitting with Jeff, Claire, and Lucas. After some good conversation, the meals were finished. While dessert was served, George made his way to the time capsule. He asked the audience, "Are you ready to see what has been hidden inside of this time capsule for all these years?" Then with a round of applause, his question was answered.

# The First Time Capsule Reading

With the assistance of Jacob and Noah, George opened the time capsule, removing the first item. George said, "The first item of the night is a journal." George held it up for all to see. Then he said, "This journal is from the late pastor Daniel Edwards." He paused as he opened it and began to read the opening prayer that Daniel had written:

> My dearest Lord and Heavenly Father, this day, I beckon unto You my solemn thoughts and prayer. On this very ground, I kneel before You in all my reverence. I ask that You bless this land and cabin and that You pour out Your Spirit on the hearts of all that enter through the narrow gate and that You keep them in 'the Way' of the saints who walked before them, Amen.

George explained to the audience the significance of that prayer. He said, "The cabin that Daniel was referring to in his prayer is the one that Marcus and Andrea are staying in this week." Andrea looked at Claire, and both women realized that they had read that same prayer on a plaque at the ranger station just the day before. Then George explained that the residents of Edwardsville had named the town after the late Pastor Daniel Edwards. Then he read an entry from his journal, saying, "This is the testimony of Daniel Edwards. He calls this, 'A Story of Redemption—I was walking deep in sin, then I received Jesus within:'"

> This is the story of how I surrendered a life of sin and death to a life of holiness in Jesus Christ. It was a rainy Monday night, and I had just lost my job. As I walked home on that muddy dirt road, I knew the door to my room would be locked. Sure enough, as I entered the boarding house, Mr. Greenwich met me in the hallway, wanting my past due rent. I asked him in shame, "Can I just have my things, and I'll go." He unlocked my bedroom door, turning his head away from the stench of liquor. He said to me, "I've got to

139

stir the soup, and when I return, you will be gone!"
And at that, he pushed the door open to my room and
left me alone.

Going in and looking at my life's worth that was
strewn around my room, I grabbed this and that,
stuffing my bag, trying not to stumble. As I turned to
leave, my eye caught the book ole widow Weber gave
me the day I moved in. She said, "This is the Lord's
book, and it will serve you well. One day you will
need to repent and surrender your life to God." I had
placed it on the dresser by the door, never giving it
another thought. I had been warned about her before I
made it to the top of the stairs when I moved into the
boarding house. One of the residents said to me in a
scratchy voice, "Watch out for that old bag. She'll try
and convert you to her Jesus." I wasn't about to let her
or her preaching into my room. Looking back, I know
that she was praying for me after she handed me that
Bible. I heard the first part as she turned and walked
away. She said, "My dearest Lord and Heavenly
Father, this day, I beckon unto You…" After I picked
up the Bible, I saw out of the corner of my eye a small
cloud of dust, reminding me that I had never picked it
up and read it, not even once.

Having nowhere to go, I made it to the edge of
town. Once there, I sat under an overhang on an
elevated loading dock behind the Lost Souls Tavern.
The rain had settled to a light drizzle, and the harsh
wind penetrated my jacket. Setting on an old bar stool,
I turned my back to the cold wind. I opened that Bible
and began to read, having only a dimly lit dock light
above my head to see by. Reading that Bible was the
only way I was able to suppress my hunger that night.
Then I read these words: *{The word is nigh thee, even
in thy mouth, and in thy heart:} {Whosoever believeth
on him shall not be ashamed.} {For whosoever shall*

*call upon the name of the Lord shall be saved.}* [KJV] ([17] Romans 10:8-13).

Soon after reading that passage, three men came out of the tavern and… Well, they beat me up pretty bad. All I had left in this world was that Bible; that was the only thing they didn't take from me. So, I opened it again and read this passage: *{The Son of man must be delivered into the hands of sinful men, and be crucified, and the third day rise again.}* [KJV] (Luke 24:7). I had never been to church, but even I knew there was a man named Jesus, but that night I came to the realization that He died for me, a sinner. But even then, I said in my heart, "Not now, Lord, not now!!" I felt a cold breeze on my back that seemed to penetrate my heart. At that moment, I knew rejecting the call of the Spirit was going to encapsulate my heart in a block of ice. I said to myself, "It's time to repent." I didn't really know what that meant at the time, but I knew I must do it and do it now. Then I walked down those loading dock steps, and at the bottom, I hesitated. That was the moment that I knew in my heart, mind, and soul that if I walked away from the altar that God had prepared for me, my journey to salvation was going to be a long and desperate road. As I was walking away, I stopped and turned around. When my eyes caught that bottom step again, knowing that God had prepared it as an altar for me, I ran back and knelt down at that makeshift altar and poured my heart out to Jesus Christ, laying all my sins at the foot of the cross. I confessed them boldly to Jesus, and that night He became my savior. As the cold wind blew in my face, my heart warmed, melting the chilling darkness that had tormented my life, mind, and soul.

As I knelt there on that step, a strange thing happened to me. With my head bowed, I said to God: on my knees: "Dear God, I am so ashamed of my life and my sin. I'm not sure if I even know how to repent, but I have to try." I began to tremble. Then I began to weep. I not only wept, but I wept bitterly, crying in anguish. I'm not sure how long this went on, but I suppose no longer than half an hour. I had expected that I would say some words or phrases in my repentance. As it turned out, when my heart took over, I just cried and wept before the Lord at that makeshift altar, not saying a single word.

I had said words in the past, but they were all lies. I had lied to my own heart, telling myself I would be a Christian. But on that night, my mind had no say in the matter; I had turned my life over to my heart and my soul. They took over, not caring what my mind wanted. It was a beautiful thing. I felt as if the Lord had said to my heart, "I am with you, My child." That was all it took for me that night. I wept until I could weep no more. When I had finished weeping, I stood up, and peace flowed through me like a pure river of life, and I knew that I had been born again and that I was a child of God.

Many years later, I was on my knees, praying when the Lord spoke to me and said, "Daniel, I want you to build me a church." That same day, I took all my savings, bought a parcel of land, and drew up plans to build the Church in the Way. The years of sin had taken a toll on my body, and I soon became ill. I persisted through hardships praying on the future building site of the church.

While I was building the Church in the Way, I became sick. Before I was able to finish, my illness started to overtake me. As I prayed, I had only one thought: that I might touch others as the ole widow Weber had touched me with her kind words and prayers. She had said, "Daniel, one day, the Lord is going to get ahold of you, and then and only then will you fall to your knees in repentance."

This may be the last entry in my journal: The Church in the Way is better than halfway complete. I can only pray that the Lord will make a way for all who enter this cabin to come to know Jesus. Father, I pray that Your spirit will be poured out on the hearts of all that enter through the narrow gate and that you will keep them in the Way of the saints who walked before them.

Signed Daniel Edwards

George wiped the tears from his eyes and said, "I wasn't expecting that. I think we could end the evening on that note, but there are still two more items to be presented."

# The Second Time Capsule Reading

Then George asked Noah, "Son, would you like to reach into the time capsule and pull out the next item?" Without any hesitation, Noah pulled out the next item, handing it to George. He said, "It looks like this is a speech from a great revivalist from yesteryear." George informed the audience that this item was not signed. Then he began to read the second item of the night:

Early in my Christian life, as I walked along the path that God had set before me, I began to notice that my foot would sometimes veer off into the grass. I paid no attention to this initially. Soon though, I noticed one foot was always in the grass. And again, before long, my other foot had also veered off the straight and narrow path. Again, I thought nothing of this. Later, I looked down at my feet, and they were both off the narrow way. I could still see the narrow path that I had been walking on. I remember thinking to myself, "I'm okay as long as I can still see the narrow way that God had provided for me." It was then that I began to look around and found that I had wandered away from the straight and narrow way that the Lord had set before me. I was lost somewhere in the forest, and I could no longer see the narrow way. The trees were magnificent. The pines were tall and straight, and the oaks were full and thick. I thought what a pleasant view. After a long while, as I strolled along, I stumbled. As I fell to the ground, I thought I had stepped into a hole. But as I tried to stand, I realized that I was lying in the muck, and my foot had not stepped into a hole, but rather, I had stepped knee-deep in that muck. Not only had I left the narrow path, but I had also left the forest. I grabbed ahold of the vines that were around me, soon becoming entangled in them, unable to move.

As I lay in the mud and the muck, with the vines wrapped around me, I looked up and saw a vision of heaven, and Jesus was sitting on His Father's throne. He said to me, "Son, why have you wandered so far from Me? You have become conformed to the world, being entangled in the vines and in the muck. Look around you and see the sin that is in your life." Then I looked and beheld the mud and the muck that I was in. It was a representation of my life of sin. I had begun to think that I could cleanse the mud from my face with the muck. The vines were binding me to the sin that was far from the narrow way that had been my life prior. Whenever I grabbed the vines, I would pull them down upon me, further entangling me in them. Then the Lord spoke to me again, saying, "Son, you are in danger of being blotted out of My book as you have denied My Holy Spirit and Me before men. If you continue in your ways, I will say to you on judgment day, 'depart from Me, I never knew you,' and I will deny you before My Father and His angels. *Do not be conformed to this world, but be transformed by the renewing of your mind, that you can prove what the will of God is for your life.*"

At that moment, I knew that I was no longer on the narrow path that the Lord had set before me. When I was, my burden was light, and my way was straight. Then I knew I must present my body as a living sacrifice, holy, acceptable to God, which is my reasonable service (Romans 12:1-2).

Immediately in my spirit, I began to cry out to Jesus, saying, "My Lord, *blessed is the man who walks not in the counsel of the ungodly. Nor who stands in the path of sinners. Nor who sits in the seat of the scornful. But his delight is in the law of the LORD, and in His law, he meditates day and night. He shall be like a tree planted by the rivers of water, that brings forth its fruit in its season, whose leaf also shall not wither; and whatever he does shall prosper. The ungodly are not so but are like the dust which the wind drives away to destruction. Therefore the ungodly shall not stand in the judgment, nor sinners in the congregation of the righteous. For the LORD knows the way of the righteous, but the way of the ungodly shall perish."* (Psalms 1:1-6).

My cry made its way to the throne room of God (Hebrews 4:14-16). Again I looked up to heaven, and I saw in my vision the Lord Jesus putting down the book of life, and He said to me, "Son, you have chosen well. *Blessed is he whose transgression is forgiven, whose sin is covered. Blessed is the man to whom the LORD does not impute iniquity, And in whose spirit there is no deceit."* And God heard the cry of my heart when I said, "*I acknowledged my sin to You, and my iniquity I have not hidden. I have confessed my transgressions to You LORD, and You forgave the iniquity of my sin"* Psalms 32:5).

Then once again, I looked down at my feet, and I was back on the path of righteousness. Having nothing to offer the Lord Jesus Christ, I offered Him my broken self, and He accepted my offering. I had finally become humbled and broken. Once again, my feet were on a firm foundation; I was back on the straight and narrow way. I had called upon the Name of the Lord, and He heard my cry. He has made me accepted in the beloved.

Later that night, I wrote in my journal, "Revival starts in the heart of man and is completed in the covenant work of God. My God has said, *I will put My laws in their mind and write them on their hearts; and I will be their God, and they shall be My people.*" Then I responded: *"There is One thing I have desired of the LORD, That will I seek: That I may dwell in the house of the LORD All the days of my life, To behold the beauty of the LORD, And to inquire in His temple."* (Matthew 12:31-32, Matthew 7:21-23, Matthew 10:32-33, [18] Romans 12:1-2, Psalms 1:1-6, Psalms 32:1-2, Matthew 7:13-14, Hebrews 8:10, Psalms 27:4).

Then in a whisper, Marcus looked at Lucas and asked, "Was that man even saved?" Lucas answered, "He was born of the Spirit at the end, thus giving him the right to be called a child of God." Then Marcus asked him, "How could someone so vile be given another chance to go to heaven?" Again Lucas answered by saying, *"For God so loved the world that He gave His only begotten Son, that whoever believes in Him should not perish but have everlasting life."* And at that, Marcus said, "Okay, okay," having a slight hint of acceptance. Then Marcus began to process all that he had heard that night. (John 1:12-13; 3:3; 3:5; 3:16).

Then Andrea, having heard what Marcus whispered to Lucas, remembered those words that she heard in her head while walking from the pavilion to the cabin earlier that day: 'ANDREA—ANDREA! MARCUS WILL NEVER COME TO THE SAVING KNOWLEDGE OF JESUS CHRIST!' Then Andrea looked across the table at Claire and remembered how that she had the baptism of repentance flowing over her the other day. Claire had said, "I'll take the faith route." Claire came to the saving knowledge of Jesus Christ that day. So, with boldness, Andrea said in her heart, "I will test that spirit, to see whether it is of God. By this, I will know the Spirit of God: *Every spirit that confesses that Jesus Christ has come in the flesh is of God"* (I John 4:1-6).

Then she said in her heart, again with boldness, "Marcus, My husband, will come to the saving knowledge of Jesus Christ, Amen!" George looked at the crowd and said, "That was a powerful testimony. God really got ahold of that man." George looked at the audience and asked, "Is God touching your hearts like He is touching mine tonight?"

# The Third Time Capsule Reading

Again George wiped away the tears, then he said, "There's one more item in the time capsule. Should we wait until tomorrow to find out what it is?" As the audience responded with a unanimous no. George asked Jacob, "Sir, would you please reach into the time capsule for the last item of the night." And at that, Jacob reached his hand into the time capsule, drew out the last article, and handed it to George. As he did, a note fell from it onto the floor. Jacob reached down and picked it up, and gave it to George. Reading it, George said: this looks like a little poem:

> I bow my knee before the Lord of Heaven. And I sing hal-le-lu-jah. And I wait for heaven's response. And They sang hal-le-lu-jah. Then I sing hal-le-lu-jah; my prayer has been received. I say: "Heaven and hope are on the rise. Let your hope be made manifest. Awake out of sleep; *for now, our salvation is nearer than when we first believed. Therefore let us cast off the works of darkness and let us put on the armor of light. Let us walk properly, as in the day, not in revelry and drunkenness, not in lewdness and lust, not in strife and envy. But put on the Lord Jesus Christ, and make no provision for the flesh, to fulfill its lusts"* ([19] Romans 13:11-14).

After reading the poem, George said, "We should all expect heaven to respond to our prayer. Now that's a walk of faith." Then George began to read the final item of the night, saying: "This is a letter on prayer by David Barnardo to Daniel Edwards. As many of you may already know, David Barnardo was an associate of Daniel Edwards. He was also Daniel's mentor in the Lord." Then George began to read:

To Daniel Edwards, a word of advice on prayer: Daniel, when I pray, I close my door, and I pray in my secret place, and my Father in heaven rewards me openly. I don't pray vain repetitions as others do. For my Father knows the things that I need even before I ask Him. So, in this manner, I pray: *Our Father in heaven, Hallowed be Your name. Your kingdom come. Your will be done On earth as it is in heaven* (Matthew 6:5-15).

You see, the Word of God is a discerner of the thoughts and intents of my heart (Hebrews 4:12). And this is the very reason that I consistently pray and ask God to examine me and try my heart because my thoughts are always before Him. I remind myself of this daily, and I even leave my heart open before the Lord of heaven. I have trained myself to remember that my thoughts are always before the Lord (Psalms 26:1-3).

We must strive to enter that place where we come humbled and broken before God seeking repentance. Now, Daniel, remember, our flesh is weak, so let us always ask Jesus, "Search me, and know my heart." (Psalms 139:23-24).

Above all else, Daniel, always, always, and again I say always, lay your heart before the throne of grace daily as an offering so Jesus can lead you in the way everlasting.

Your friend and teacher in the Lord

David Barnardo

After George finished that last time capsule reading, a few townspeople turned their lives over to Jesus Christ, becoming born again that night. Soon after, George said farewell to all the guests who came out to share the event. As everyone began to leave for the night, Andrea had one thought that had been playing on her mind. She asked herself, "Was that hard shell of a heart of Marcus finally beginning to crack?" **Then Andrea received a word from the Lord in her spirit: "Andrea, this is the instruction on the**

**beautiful one—the tree of life. Andrea, the evidence that Marcus is a child of God will be when he professes that My Son is his Lord and Savior."**
**Discussion Questions:**

1) You have read in the first time capsule reading: *"Whoever calls on the name of the LORD shall be saved."* In what manner of spirit should an individual be calling upon the name of the Lord?

    Answer: *The LORD is near to those who have a broken heart, And saves such as have a contrite spirit.* (Psalms 34:18, Isaiah 66:2).

2) You have read in the second time capsule reading: Revival starts in the heart of man and is completed in the covenant work of God. You may have seen revivals on TV or even read about them throughout history. What does revival look like to you?

    See also: Hebrews 8:7-13, II Corinthians 3:3.

3) You have read in the third time capsule reading: The Word of God is a discerner of the thoughts and intents of my heart, found in Hebrews 4:12. Are you willing to put your heart on the altar of God and have Him read and discern your heart daily? Are you ready to pray the prayer of Psalms 26:1-3?

    Answer: Found within your heart.

Scriptures: Romans 8:37, Romans 10:8-13, Luke 24:7, Hebrews 4:14-16, Psalms 32:5, Matthew 12:31-32, Matthew 7:21-23, Matthew 10:32-33, Romans 12:1-2, Psalms 1:1-6, Psalms 32:1-2, Matthew 7:13-14, Hebrews 8:10, Psalms 27:4, [John 1:12-13; 3:3; 3:5; 3:16], I John 4:1-6, Romans 13:11-14, Matthew 6:5-15, Hebrews 4:12, Psalms 26:1-3, Psalms 139:23-24.

Discussion Question Scriptures: Psalms 34:18, Isaiah 66:2, Hebrews 8:7-13, II Corinthians 3:3, Hebrews 4:12, Psalms 26:1-3.

# Chapter 23 ~ Sunday

# Knock—Knock

This was the first morning in a long time that Marcus found himself waking up with the sun shining on his face, not having to rise so early and go to work. With this project now completed, a moment of peace began to flow over him. He thought, "My honeymoon has finally begun." Then he said, "Andrea, honey, where are you?" Rising from his bed, Marcus made his way to the kitchen. Seeing Andrea had already made coffee, he poured himself a cup. Sitting down at the table, he took a sip and was surprised that it was cold. Marcus was puzzled. He knew that neither he nor Andrea had made coffee the night before. Then he found a note laying on the table:

Marcus, I've gone seeking the truth!

Love Andrea

With the note in hand, Marcus asked himself, "What could this possibly mean?" After searching the cabin and the area immediately outside, Marcus began the twenty-minute hike to the ranger station, searching for Andrea. As he walked, Marcus thought, "It sure is a little chilly out here this morning." With that thought, Marcus finally realized that he had a problem being honest with himself. Then he finally admitted the truth, saying aloud. "It's not just chilly; it's downright cold out here!" With that thought, Marcus flipped the collar up on his coat and put his hands in his pockets. Continuing his trek to the ranger station, Marcus hoped that he had not just lost the love of his life. He questioned himself, "Last night, I ripped my heart open, entrusting my most endearing secret to my best friend, my wife, Andrea." He began to wonder how it was that he could finely open up, telling Andrea that story that he had guarded for so long. As he crossed the red covered bridge, Marcus thought, "For the first time since that dreadful day, I feel a glimmer of hope that it may be possible to be free of this guilty conscience that I carry."

Thoughts began flowing through his mind of his crew's honesty and sincerity throughout this project. There was Lucas's heartwarming story of the tragic loss of his wife and how he held to his faith in God. Then Noah and his testimony. Marcus thought, "I could see in his eyes how God had taken away all the shame of his time in prison." As he walked the trail with the ranger station in sight, Marcus stopped dead in his tracks. He thought, "Keith's story sure brought tears to my eyes yesterday evening." Marcus was still reeling in amazement that Keith could offer forgiveness in the wake of all that happened to him.

After arriving at the ranger station, Marcus noticed that his truck was gone, and he knew that Andrea must have taken it. Then finding all the doors still locked at the ranger station, he sat on a bench outside as a feeling of despair and hopelessness had taken hold of him. A moment of honesty gripped his mind, and he admitted to himself that he knew good and well what Andrea's note had meant. Now with his face in his hands, he said, "Lord, please, all that I want in this world is to have Andrea as my wife." Just then, another one of those hooded men walked by him, saying with the voice of hope, "Marcus, make your paths straight." Then a peaceful presence flowed over him. Looking up and seeing no one, Marcus remembered the discussion that he had with Jacob the day before:

> "Marcus, we need to come to Jesus in our brokenness.
> It's this way because we rejected Him as Adam did in
> the garden of Eden. We must recognize that we are
> the ones who walked away from God. You see, the

Lord never rejected us; He merely reacted to our disobedience. God never stopped loving us, but He had to keep to His word. That is why God sent the man and the woman out of the garden. That was to preserve His word and His way. We are to come back to him through repentance and brokenness of heart. The word of God tells us that the Lord Jesus will not refuse us when we come to Him broken and contrite. It is God who accepts us, as we are the ones that walked away from Him in the first place. When you're ready, come broken before Jesus, and he will accept you. Marcus, keep this thought in mind, it was God who came calling for Adam and Eve in the garden of Eden after they ate the fruit of the tree of the knowledge of good and evil. Oh, and remember, we must weep over our sins being remorseful in our prayer like we find throughout the book of Psalms." (Genesis 3, Psalm 102:17).

Marcus sat there on that old hardwood bench, pondering those words for what seemed like hours with his head down, when all of a sudden, he felt a hand pressing on his shoulder. "Hey, are you okay, Boss?" Lucas asked. "Yes, I'm fine," Marcus said. Then he immediately recognized that was not true. He said, "No, Lucas, I'm not fine. I told her everything last night, and I didn't leave anything out. I even fell to my knees, telling her I was sorry for not being honest with her."

Marcus went into great detail about his situation, telling Lucas everything he had told Andrea the night before. Then Marcus said, "I woke up this morning finding Andrea gone. Not knowing what else to do, I came here hoping to find her." Lucas asked, "Did she seem upset with you?" "No, she was unexpectedly calm," Marcus answered. Just then, Marcus snapped his fingers and said, "I think I know where she went." "Come on, let's go find her," Lucas said while he walked to his truck. "But it's several hours away, and it's only a hunch," Marcus said while still sitting on the bench. Lucas replied, "I said, 'Let's go.'" Still waiting for Marcus to get up, Lucas emphasized, "Let's go," waving his hand several times.

As the two men walked across the parking lot, Lucas said, "Marcus, you should pray over your situation before we hit the road." "That's a good idea. What do you have in mind?" Marcus asked. "What I have in mind is you're the one that needs to pray over your situation, asking God to guide your path," Lucas said. "Okay, you know I'm not good at this, but here goes," Marcus said. Then he said, "Father God, I have done an awful thing, and all I can ask is that you will forgive me..." Interrupting him, Lucas said, "Boss, let me be clear with you. You confessed last night to Andrea. Then, this morning, you also told me everything. God has heard your confession, and he knows your heart. You need to pray that God will guide you, instructing you how to handle this situation. So, start by saying something like this: 'Our Father in heaven; Your kingdom come; Your will be done on earth as it is in heaven. You know my situation; all I ask of You is…' Now, you take it from there." Marcus was a little nervous as he's never really prayed before. He bowed his head and began to finish the prayer that Lucas started for him, saying: "All I can ask of You is that You help me to make my paths straight and send my life in a different direction. Amen." Marcus looked at Lucas and asked, "How was that?" "I didn't ask for fancy words, I just asked for heart, and that's just what you did—you gave it heart," Lucas said, then adding, "Well done."

As the two men began the long drive, Marcus soon drifted into deep thought as Keith's testimony ran through his mind once more:

## Keith's Testimony:

It wasn't until I put Jesus Christ first in my life that I could forgive my wife, Dorothy. Unbeknownst to me, she was having an affair that lasted several years. After I found out, I filed for divorce, which took longer than I had anticipated. During that time of transition, I turned to the Bible and began to read. What I found in the Gospel was nothing short of a model for my own salvation. Dorothy had violated the principles of our marriage just the same as Adam and Eve violated the relationship that they had with God

in the garden of Eden (Genesis 3:1-22). I began to see
how mankind had turned their back on God by
yielding to the temptation of that serpent. I, too, saw
how I had fallen short of the glory of God, needing
the salvation of Jesus Christ in my own life (Romans
3:21-26). Very soon after reading the Gospel accounts
of the crucifixion of Jesus Christ, I began to feel my
own sinfulness. I became humbled and broken,
calling on the name of Jesus. (Romans 10:9 & Psalms
34:18). Once the Holy Spirit filled me with the
salvation of God, I began the process of forgiving my
wife for her indiscretions. I managed to enter a season
of prayer, and I found myself continually praying over
my wife. I felt in my heart that I still loved her. Then
about six weeks after being filled with the Holy Spirit,
my wife came knocking at my door. She was standing
there on my doorstep one moment and then falling to
her knees the next. She began to weep, saying
between the sobs, "I'm sorry. I'm so sorry. Please
forgive me! Please! Please forgive me! I have made a
terrible mistake." The divorce papers were almost
finalized, and our marriage was going to be over in
less than a week. She was the perfect picture of the
baptism of repentance—contrite, humbled, and
broken (II Corinthians 7:9). Then reaching down, I
took her hand and lifted her up. I said to her, "I have
always loved you." She asked me, "Would you accept
me back as your wife?" I also began to weep as my
prayers had finally been answered—my wife had
returned to me—for our marriage was dead and is
alive again, was lost, and is found (Luke 15:11-32).
Our marriage was made new—reborn, as I like to say.
We have been back together, going on thirty years,
and raised four wonderful children.

It was years after our marriage was reconciled that
I made the connection. We surrender our life, finding
it to be worthless. Then we, through humility and

brokenness, ask God to accept us into His life. Being reconciled to Jesus is much like Dorothy being reconciled to me in our marriage.

As Lucas turned off the interstate, he asked, "Hey, are you okay? You were in a daze." Marcus answered, "Yes, I'm okay. I was just thinking about Keith's testimony." Then Lucas turned the truck onto another highway, and the two men continued on their journey. Marcus and Lucas were halfway there. Soon enough, Marcus slipped back into another daydream. He was thinking about one of the talks he had with Noah while working around the mine.

## Noah's Testimony:

Marcus remembered Noah saying: While He hung on the cross, Jesus became sin for you and me so that we could become right with God. When someone belongs to Christ, they have become a new person, having received the Holy Spirit and a virtuous heart. As Jesus was about to die, he said, "I thirst!" And then, "It is finished." After that, He gave up His Spirit. Later, some men took the body of Jesus and prepared Him for burial, lying Him to rest in a tomb, sealing the entrance with a stone. Then on the first day of the week, Mary discovered that the stone had been rolled away from the entrance. She went and told the disciples that Jesus was no longer in His tomb. The disciples came and looked, but eventually, they left after discovering that Jesus was gone. However, Mary stayed, and as she wept, she looked inside the tomb finding two angels where Jesus had lain. Then turning around, she saw Jesus.

This is where we look to an Old Testament prophet who said, "I will give you a new heart and put a new Spirit within you; I will take out the heart of stone and give you a heart of flesh." The resurrection of Jesus represents that the stony heart is removed, that old sin nature, leaving us with a tender new heart when we are born again. God can then guide us through His

Holy Spirit to follow His ways and do His will. One key element often missed is that God will always do His part in the salvation process. However, He also expects us to do our part. For example, roll away the stone, and the stone was rolled away. They sound the same, but the first is our responsibility, and the second is God's. Jesus made this clear in the raising of Lazarus when he told them to roll away the stone. Taking that stone out of the way was the responsibility of the people. Consequently, the resurrection of Jesus was the responsibility of God; therefore, an angel of the Lord was the one who rolled that stone away. So, in the complex issue of salvation, we have to do our part, and that is, we have to repent and have faith in God. Then God will do His part and provide us with His Holy Spirit. (II Corinthians 5:12-21, John 19:17-20:18, Ezekiel 36:25-27, John 11:38-41. Matthew 28:1-2).

"Hey Boss, we're here," said Lucas. Marcus said, "Sorry, I was daydreaming again." Then just before he got out of the truck, he said, "I hope you don't mind, but I need to do this by myself." Then Marcus walked up the driveway and stood at the front door. Knock—Knock.

**Discussion Questions:**

1) Andrea left Marcus a note that said, **"I've gone seeking the truth!"** Have you ever had a situation in your life similar to Marcus in this chapter where he became honest, telling Andrea everything that was on his heart?

2) In this chapter, Marcus recalled a testimony that Keith shared with him. What book of the Old Testament, in the minor prophets, is similar to Keith's story?
Answer: The book of Hosea.

3) Roll away the stone, and the stone was rolled away. From Noah's story: can you apply this scenario to your life?
Answer: Roll away the stone: something that you must accomplish, such as repentance; whereas: and the stone was rolled away, is something that God will accomplish for you,

such as salvation. For clarification read, John 11:39 & John 20:1.

Scriptures: Genesis 3, Psalm 102:17, Genesis 3:1-22, Romans 3:21-26, Romans 10:9, Psalms 34:18, II Corinthians 7:9, Luke 15:11-32, II Corinthians 5:12-21, John19:17-20:18, Ezekiel 36:25-27, John 11:38-41. Matthew 28:1-2.

Discussion Question Scriptures: John 11:39, John 20:1.

# Chapter 24 ~ Sunday

# You Just Need To Say It

While Marcus was standing there in the cold, he began to second guess himself by saying, "It's been over five years since I've been to Lindsay's parents' house. I'm not sure if this is even the right one." Further doubting himself, he thought, "Wasn't there a maple tree in the center of the circular driveway?" Then gaining the upper hand on uncertainty, he told himself, "Yes, I'm at the right house. I'm certain of it." He remembered that their house was the only one on the block with a circular driveway. Just then, the door opened, and a young woman said to Marcus, "May I help you, Sir?" Bringing his attention back into focus, Marcus said, "Hi Lindsey, it's me, Marcus, Marcus Peterson." "Yes, I think I remember you. Aren't you the boy from across town? Didn't we go to high school together?" Lindsay asked. As Marcus began to answer her questions, Lindsay interrupted him and said, "Come on in, Marcus, I've been expecting you this morning." As Lindsay opened the door all the way, Marcus saw Andrea sitting on the couch with a cup of coffee in her hand with a warm smile on her face. "Fancy meeting you here, honey," Andrea said. Marcus' nerves were beginning to get the best of him. He said, "Andrea, this is Lindsay Carter; she was my girlfriend back in high school." Andrea responded, "Yes, I believe we have already met." Then gesturing with her hand, Andrea patted the couch as if to say, "Come on, sit over here, next to me."

"Marcus, you look like you could use a cup of coffee," Lindsey said. "No, I don't want to impose on you," Marcus replied. Walking into the kitchen, Lindsey yelled, "What do you take in your coffee?" "He takes it black," Andrea replied, looking over her shoulder. Then she smiled at her husband, slightly easing his tension. Returning and handing him his coffee Lindsey sat down across from Marcus and asked him, "So, Marcus Peterson, what brings you to my house today?"

Looking down at the floor, Marcus was suddenly overcome with emotions as the tears began to flow from his eyes. Andrea and Lindsay joined him with tears of their own. Then Marcus began to weep. This continued for some time as that day had been reserved for his heart to be emptied out. As composure settled back into the room, Marcus began to speak. He said to Lindsay, "How could I have been so selfish, leaving you there at the clinic all by yourself." "And what clinic was that?" Lindsay asked. Then Marcus turned his head and looked into Andrea's eyes. As he did, another tear streamed down her face. Then putting her hand on his, Lindsay said, "Marcus, you just need to say it." Marcus said, "Okay, okay." Then he paused for a few moments and said, "The abortion clinic. I'm sorry that I left you at the abortion clinic all by yourself." Marcus felt the shame of his actions as he emptied his heart of his past indiscretions. Then he said, "I'm sorry that I never called or checked on you after that." Then he began to sob once more. It was a little while before he regained his composure. Then Marcus looked up at Lindsay, and she said to him: "It was you who wanted an abortion. Your parents wanted you to want an abortion. My own parents even wanted me to have an abortion, but I never wanted it. None of you would listen to what I had to say. Everyone's concern was, 'How is this baby going to affect my life?' I told you that I didn't want to have an abortion for weeks, but you never listened to me. All you could think about was football and getting your scholarship. How's your knee anyway?" "My knee is good now. I take it you know my knee injury knocked me out of the scholarship contention," Marcus said. He paused and said, "I have carried this terrible guilt of selfishness because I pressed you into getting that abortion. There is no way that I can ever make up for that. I had to come here and face you to tell you how sorry I am." Then Lindsay stood up as if to leave the room, and she yelled, "Robby! Robby, come in here, please?" Just then, Robby walked into the living room and stood next to Lindsay. She said, "Robby, I want you to meet Marcus Peterson." Then Lindsay added, "Marcus, I would like to introduce to you Robby Carter. Marcus, he is your son; this little boy is your son." And with that statement, Marcus fell to his knees and broke down. He began to weep inconsolably. That great sin of his was no longer able to hold him in bondage.

A while later, after Marcus regained his composure, Lindsey explained the events of that day, saying, "After you dropped me off at the abortion clinic, a friend was waiting for me in the parking lot to take me home. My parents, try as they may, were unable to convince me to have the abortion in the days and weeks that followed. I also refused to give the baby up for adoption. I made it clear that my mind was made up when I discovered I was pregnant. I said to myself, 'I will have this baby, and I will raise it no matter what.'" Looking back, Marcus was so grateful that Lindsay was strong enough to do the right thing amongst her adversaries.

Andrea wiped the tears from her eyes while Lindsay said, "Robby, honey, do you have anything that you would like to say to your father?" Robby looked Marcus in the eyes and said, "Every night when I say my prayers, I always say to God, 'God, one day You should give me a daddy because I need one.'" Then with a big smile, Robby gave Marcus the toy truck that he was holding. And in that smile, Marcus saw that both of Robby's front teeth had recently fallen out. Lindsay said to Robby, "I have a feeling that we are going to be seeing a lot of your daddy and Andrea. With tears still flowing, Marcus nodded his head in agreement. Andrea said, "This is a good day. This is a really good day." Then Andrea said, "Robby, you're going to get to know your daddy very well." At that, Lindsay's parents came into the living room with refreshments. Then Andrea asked, "So, Marcus, how did you get here anyway?" Marcus replied, "Lucas, I forgot all about Lucas.

**Discussion Questions:**

1) Have you ever found yourself in a situation like Marcus in this chapter? Marcus found himself outside his old girlfriend's house, and he hadn't been there in five years, not recognizing those things that were once familiar. Are there issues in your life you would like to address before they become unfamiliar?

2) In this chapter, Lindsay said to Marcus, "You just need to say it." Have you ever had a situation where you had something substantial on your mind that you just had to say? If so, can you describe what it was?

3) How do you think this chapter would have turned out if Lindsay would have had the abortion? How do you feel about abortion? Are you for it or against it?

Scriptures: none.

Discussion Question Scriptures: none.

# Chapter 25 ~ Years Later

# A Child of God ~ A Summary

Shortly after that week in Edwardsville, a light came on in Jeff's head. He remembered his dream of falling into the pit of hell, having no hope of salvation, along with his deep thirst. That time alone with Jacob at the ranger station encouraged him the most. Jacob explained Jeff's dream to him by saying, "Your sorrow was continually before you. You were ready to declare your iniquity, and you were in anguish over your sin" (Psalms 38:17-18). It was then that Jeff knew in his heart that he wanted to be mentored in the faith by Jacob. Jeff and Claire had Cliff over for dinner one night, and they phoned Jacob to ask him to mentor them along with Jim and Steve. They would all get on their computers and video chat once a week, sharing their faith. They would talk about various items that the Lord showed them when He spoke to their hearts. This mentoring lasted for several years until they were all grounded in the faith. Noah joined in with them from time to time, giving a word of encouragement. As for Claire, she contacted Andrea asking to be mentored by her. They met once a month in a ladies' Bible study.

Katie-Bird and Bruce were married a year after they met. They both had a heart for God, so they moved to the city and became missionaries.

One day Marcus told me how that first week at the cabin was the best week of his life. Then he said, "Don't get me wrong, though, the second week, the honeymoon, was great also." But it was at the end of that first week that he felt an unexplainable peace for the first time. He first saw it on Andrea after the incident down at the creek. Then he always felt it while working around Lucas, Jacob, and Noah. He even witnessed the change firsthand when it occurred in Jeff and Claire's life. "That cabin is where it all began. That's where I found the peace that surpasses understanding." Marcus would say. Marcus finally realized that his hands nailed Jesus to the cross, but that alone didn't save him. It was when he came to the realization that Jesus went to the cross to pay the price for his sin. (I Peter 1:17-21, Colossians 1:13). That's when he repented of his sins being humbled and broken, calling on the name of the Lord, receiving the gift of the Holy Spirit. (Acts 2:36-39, Psalms 51:17). It was then that Marcus professed that Jesus Christ was Lord of his life. Thus fulfilling the word of the Lord that Andrea received in her spirit after the dinner and time capsule readings that Saturday night. That's when Andrea's prayers were answered when Marcus understood what he read in *The Way News Journal* that said, *'Andrea, our heavenly Father, is drawing your husband to the Son of God.'* Afterward, Marcus was on the path to feed his family spiritually from the beautiful one—the tree of life.

Marcus and Andrea's son Jason grew up and became a successful businessman in the community. He married his girlfriend, Debbie Johnson. Marcus and Andrea had a great relationship with his first son Robby Carter and his mother, Lindsay. Marcus and Lucas are still friends today and have worked together on other projects in Edwardsville. Years later, Lucas figured out who that hooded man was down at the sandy beach. The one he saw walking away when Andrea almost drowned in the creek. However, he kept it to himself.

One of the most significant days in the life of Marcus Peterson was when he had the privilege of introducing his son Jason to his baby sister Katie. Marcus looked into the eyes of his beautiful brand-new baby girl. He said to her from his heart, "Katie, don't talk to strangers, don't get into a car with someone you don't know, and above all else, always let your mother and I know where you are."

It was Claire who found that ancient Indian arrowhead as they walked past the small rockpile down by the creek when she and Andrea hiked to the miners' village. Claire, not knowing at the time that the arrowhead was instrumental in Andrea's near-drowning, gave it to her as a gift after she heard about Andrea's story. When Katie was born, Andrea gave Marcus the arrowhead to celebrate him becoming the father of a baby girl. Later in life, Andrea gave the black box that she found underneath the rocks to her daughter Katie, which said 'A Mothers Love' engraved in gold lettering. This unfailing family love inspired Katie to grow up becoming a talented young woman.

I can attest to Marcus Peterson's story. My name is Drew Carter, and I am Robby Carter's daughter and Marcus' granddaughter. Many lives were changed and influenced by Marcus becoming the man of God he was called to be. And the Spirit and the bride say, "Come!" (Revelation 22:17).
Scriptures: Psalms 38:17-18, I Peter 1:17-21, Colossians 1:13, Acts 2:36-39, Psalms 51:17, Revelation 22:17.

# Chapter 26 ~ Many Years Later

# The Cabin in the Deep Dark Woods ~ Epilogue

They had been friends since grade school, even attending each other's weddings. They made a pact on the playground one day back in the second grade, and they all agreed that they would take a vacation together before they turned fifty years old. Jimmy Stone had never forgotten that commitment. So he organized that trip, even paying for two of his childhood friends to attend, Tony Clark and Jack Dillon. Scott Wilson had declined the invitation, but a week before the trip, Scott was laid-off from work and decided that you just can't put a price tag on a vacation. Kevin Martin, the oldest of the gang, his birthday was at the end of September last year, and he is the only one who had already turned 50.

As the truck rounded the bend, Jack yelled, "Hey, there it is." Then Jimmy turned into the cabin's parking lot. They parked the truck next to the new mailbox with the address 1224 Sandrock Creek Boulevard written on the side. All five men exited the truck grabbing their gear and supplies. Jimmy said, "Guys, we're taking the first marked trail to the cabin." This trip had been on and off several times during the past few months. Two of the men, Tony and Jack, had a tough year. Tony lost his son to a drug overdose.

Jack and his wife just separated again. The hike was quiet, and they were getting reacquainted as this was the first time the gang had been back together in nine years. Jimmy was doing better than the rest of his friends. He is a member of the city council, but even he has his secrets. Soon they arrived at the cabin, and everyone claimed a bed.

Kevin was the first one to make his way into the kitchen. He worked the night shift as a security guard the night before and had decided to make some coffee to help keep him awake. The others were unpacking and organizing when Kevin sat down at the table with his fresh cup of coffee. He noticed someone had left a book on the table. He read from the book's front cover, "The Cabin in the Deep Dark Woods, written by Drew Carter." Just then, Scott asked the group, "Hey, what's the weather supposed to be like this week?" Kevin said, "Storms tomorrow and rain until Thursday." Kevin was already on page 3.

None of the men on that trip had spent any time in prayer, not even Tony after the death of his son. As Kevin flipped the pages in the book, a passage caught his eye: "One day, you will need to repent and surrender your life to God." [from chapter 22] At that, Kevin shut the book, and a flash of lightning lit up the sky. Then the thunder roared like the Lion of the Tribe of Juda.

**Discussion Question:**

1) Sometimes in life, people are dealt a different hand of cards. Though once equal in grade school, the five men on that trip were in very different economic and social settings. Although those differences were significant, they all lack a prayer life and a relationship with Jesus Christ. The statement in this chapter: ("One day you will need to repent and surrender your life to God.") is the one thing they all lacked. After reading this book, have you repented and surrendered your life to Jesus Christ?

   Answer: Hebrews 4:12 For the word of God is living and powerful, and sharper than any two-edged sword, piercing even to the division of soul and spirit, and of joints and marrow, and is a discerner of the thoughts and intents of the heart.

# Thank You from the Author

Thank you for purchasing *The Cabin in the Deep Dark Woods 2—The Spirit and the Bride.* As a special gift, I would like to send you a free PDF of the *Non-Believer's Challenge*—a sixty-day study. To receive your free copy, send an email to:

**TheCabin@turnifyouwill.org**
**TheCabinInTheDeepDarkWoods.com**

I hope you enjoyed your stay at the Cabin in the Deep Dark Woods. Please be sure to visit again by reading the other books in the series:

**The Cabin in the Deep Dark Woods—*A Discerner of the Heart.***
**The Cabin in the Deep Dark Woods 3—*Lost in the Way.*** Release date late 2022.

**Other books by the author:**
**Ye Three Men—*You are an Epistle of Christ.***
**Ye Three Men Devotional Edition: *Devotional with Scripture.***
Thank you
Tim Barker